Awakening Anne

KALYNN APPLEWHITE

ISBN: 979-8-9883558-0-9

First Edition April 2023.

Cover Art by Maria Dimova
Illustrations by Kalynn Applewhite

For Zack,
My Love. Forever.

"To upset the conclusion that all crows are black, there is no need to seek demonstration that no crows are black; it is sufficient to produce one white crow. A single one is sufficient."

- William James, American Society for Psychical Research (1890)

CHAPTER

1

DR. CUTLER LOOKED TO his wife, still wearing the same frayed black dress she had worn since their son's funeral. Being her only garment in the grim color, Mrs. Cutler had refused to wear anything else, even to their niece's wedding the week before. On particularly somber mornings, she could be seen wearing the accompanying hat. The same hat coincidentally that her mother had worn to her father's funeral when their son was only a baby. Nine years of sitting in the moth ridden wardrobe had done much to worsen the already garish head covering, and Dr. Cutler was sure he had never seen anything uglier.

As they stepped from the cab, he grimaced as many from the street stared at the dismal eyesore atop his wife's head. It was black, of course, with the remains of a sickly, dead bird staring bizarrely in opposite directions. Beneath it, damaged lace frills surrounded what appeared to be the clippings of a poor rose garden. The climax to the depressing bonnet was a crinkled black veil serving to cover the face of the unfortunate wearer from the eyes of those passing by.

Dr. Cutler had taken his wife out on this particular morning in the hopes of staging a coup against the dress, the hat, and most importantly, the dark cloud that had overtaken his once cheery partner. Perhaps to even let some light back into their home. Being a doctor himself and therefore a practical man by nature, Dr. Cutler had truly come to the end of his ideas when he called on a Ms. Maggie Barlow. He had come across her advertisement in the morning paper as his poor wife sniffled over her tea. In an act of admitted desperation, he had written to the given address, receiving a prompt response for an appointment to be held in two days' time.

The news of what he had done brought the first gleam of happiness to his wife's eyes that he had seen in many weeks. At that very moment, he had realised the gravity of this appointment, and that if it did not live up to his wife's growing expectations, the consequences could be utterly catastrophic. But, despite his own misgivings, he could hardly disappoint her now.

Dr. Cutler hurried his wife inside number 321 Warren Street, New York, New York, as it had said in the advertisement, hoping not only to avoid one of his patients, or Heaven forbid a colleague, from seeing a man of his position on such an unusual consultation but also to limit the public's exposure to his wife's hat.

Inside the textured glass door was a dimly lit hall with doors marked 319 and 320 on either side. Ahead of them stretched a set of narrow wooden stairs crowned at the top with a light fixture which produced a dim green glow through the colored glass encasing. The strange light gave the passage an eerie sense. Dr. Cutler cleared his throat loudly as if to ward off such silly premonitions and led his wife up the stairs where he found the door marked 321 waiting for them.

He stood outside the door a moment, reluctant to disturb the quiet. Somehow, now that he had arrived, he felt a nagging desire to return home, the prospect of their unusual appointment now becoming more ominous than before. Of course, this whole line of apprehensive thought left him feeling rather silly. Dr. Cutler decided that it was not nerves that kept him from entering the room before him but that the whole idea had been ludicrous to begin with, and he'd rather save his time anyway.

"Won't you open it, dear?" Mrs. Cutler asked quietly from behind him.

She had lifted the dreary veil. For the first time in a long while, Dr. Cutler saw past her morbid ensemble and into his wife's bright eyes, the same feature which had drawn him across the room eleven years ago and down the aisle that next summer.

"Of course," he said with an absent smile.

Dr. Cutler reached out his hand and was quite surprised as the doorknob turned itself in his grasp. He released the knob as suddenly as if it were a venomous insect. The door opened, revealing the face of a rather beautiful young woman.

"Very sorry to startle you," she said in a welcoming voice, to Dr. Cutler's embarrassment. She studied them both with light green eyes which complimented her pale coloring. In contrast, her hair was dark and rich, pinned up in an efficient yet stylish way. A string of pearls hung from her neck, gathered in a knot over her silk blouse.

"Not at all," he said, lowering his voice and raising himself to his full height.

"Please come in," she said, opening the door wider to admit them.

"I am right to assume you are Ms. Barlow?" he asked, removing his hat and stepping into the parlor.

Within, the room was fitted with thick purple curtains which obscured all signs of light and life from the world beyond. In fact, the only light whatsoever came from three dim lamps on the walls. In the center of the room was a table of odd sorts as well, for on its surface two words were carefully carved, yes and no, separated by an arrow that was fixed at the center. A wardrobe loomed behind the table topped with three stuffed crows surveying them all from above as if there was still life in them yet.

"That is correct," Maggie said, "and you are here about your son, as I recall?"

"Yes, that's right," Mrs. Cutler added quietly, stepping through the door after her husband.

4

Dr. Cutler glanced at his wife, taken quite pleasantly by surprise that the usual fit of tears did not follow this mention of their son.

"And what was your son's name, Mrs. Cutler?" Maggie asked as she followed the couple into the parlor.

"Simon Paul," she answered, her gaze occupied by the strange surroundings. "Named for my grandfather. He passed just before Paulie was born."

"Is that what you called him in life?" Maggie asked.

"We all called him Paulie," Mrs. Cutler said, nodding as she wiped a tear with her handkerchief.

Dr. Cutler tightened his grip on her hand as a reassurance. However, his focus had fallen on the trio of crows perched atop the wardrobe. He found himself locked in their unsettling gaze.

"Dr. Cutler, before we begin, if you would be so kind as to restrain me," Maggie instructed as she rounded the table to her usual seat.

He turned toward her with an odd expression, certain his absent mind had caused him to mishear her. "Beg your pardon?" he said, but she did not respond. Instead, Maggie sat lightly down in the chair closest to the old wardrobe and looked up at him expectantly.

It was not at all like the other three chairs circling the table, which were all comfortably upholstered. The chair was wooden, its arms fashioned with straps to secure the wrists. Further inspection revealed restraints to bind the ankles as well. For extra measure, the chair's legs had been bolted to the floor. Surely such an odd, almost unsettling, furnishing would be more likely found in an asylum than a parlor, but it was a peculiar parlor after all.

After an eagerly reassuring look from his wife, Dr. Cutler took the straps in hand and, after a bit of coaching, fastened them into place. Maggie was patient with the process. Most of the gentlemen who came for appointments required some encouragement, afraid to damage her delicate frame with too much force. However, once he managed to bind her properly, Maggie was at last able to focus her mind on the task at hand.

"If you will take your seats, we can begin," Maggie invited.

Dr. and Mrs. Cutler sat tentatively around the table. Maggie smiled to herself. It was always the same with those who came to her doors. The subtle fears which surfaced in even the greatest skeptics when the room grew dark and quiet. But always greater than their apprehension was the curiosity which kept them rooted to their seats. Maggie often wondered if their unease came from something more, that feeling as they approached the curtain which divided the material from the unseen, the closeness that had followed her for most of her life. Could they feel it now as she could, like a mist hovering in the air?

"Now, please join hands," Maggie instructed. "Attempting to contact the spirits can be a physical experience. Please do not be frightened," Maggie imparted in a serious voice. They heeded her words, each taking one of her hands and joining their own over the table. "Mrs. Cutler, if you would call out to your son. A familiar voice will do best to draw him to us. Try to ask only questions with yes or no answers to begin, please. He should be able to answer even if his presence is weak."

Dr. Cutler looked to his wife, utterly unsure of what was about to happen, and swallowed heavily.

"Paulie," Mrs. Cutler called, her round eyes wide, looking about the room for the smallest sign of another in their midst. "It's Mommy. Are you here?"

Maggie's mind reached out, beyond her body, through the misty curtain.

They waited in the quiet lamplight for an answer, but there was nothing but silence. A weight lifted from Dr. Cutler's shoulders. Somehow the quiet reassured him. This had been just a foolish venture after all. Surely he had never truly expected to hear from his departed son in some dark apartment on Warren Street.

"Paulie," she called again. "Can you hear us? Can you answer?"

Dr. Cutler froze as the arrow on the table began to twitch. The room went silent as the twitching became an unmistakable jerk. Maggie's hands were still secure in their grips and her feet were still restrained against the chair, yet the arrow on the table continued to teeter and wag. Then it stopped. Yes.

"Dear God," Mrs. Cutler exclaimed in a whisper barely more audible than a breath. She clutched Dr. Cutler's hand until his fingers went as red as his face was white.

"Is that really you?" Dr. Cutler asked desperately, unable to stop himself.

A twitch, then, yes.

"His presence is growing," Maggie said, eyes clenched and mind focused.

She could feel him drifting nearer. The sensation grew as Maggie ventured further, following his whispers and leaving the safety of her own body behind. The hairs on her neck rose as her skin chilled. Her breath shivered. The whispers came to her clearly, not as words, but as feelings, memories.

"Are you happy?" Mrs. Cutler asked.

"He wants you to know that he is not alone. He is with someone," Maggie said. Her eyes opened wide, though her focus was far away. "A man, no, a boy..."

"Is it Peter?" Mrs. Cutler gasped, now clinging to her husband's arm.

"They play together, the best of friends," Maggie continued.

This sent Mrs. Cutler into another gush of tears.

"He tells me something upset him before his death, something he wanted that was denied. It troubles you still, but he feels no anger toward you."

Mrs. Cutler said something incoherent through her now inconsolable sobs.

"Ask him," Dr. Cutler began slowly, taking advantage of his own turn to speak, "was I a good father? Did I give him the love a father should?"

Maggie concentrated. His consciousness floated away like vapor. She followed him until she could feel the boundary wisp icily against her skin. Her body shook beyond her control. The arrow on the table began spinning wildly. Around them, the lamp lights flickered and dimmed. The Cutlers looked to her in alarm.

"Her pulse!" Dr. Cutler exclaimed. "She's having a fit!"

Suddenly the movement ceased. Maggie's breath came ragged, emitting puffs of fog. The darkness swallowed her mind, but she could hear his every word as clearly as if they were speaking face to face.

"Father?" she whispered, echoing the boy's words.

"Yes, Paulie, speak to us!" Mrs. Cutler exclaimed, nearly leaping to her feet.

He spoke on so quickly. It took every bit of focus to hear him as the chill crowded her senses. "I hear him..." It was too cold, too empty. Soon she could sustain it no longer.

Maggie jolted as she returned to the parlor, to her own body. The cold was replaced with nothing but a clamminess in her skin. The mist had lifted, whispers silent. "I'm sorry. I've lost the connection." Maggie said, sounding quite faint. "If you would be so kind as to release me."

Dr. Cutler attended to the straps immediately, looking at the young woman's weak expression, wondering if she would be requiring his physician's skill.

"Thank you very much," Maggie said, remaining in her seat. Dr. Cutler returned to his, bringing his chair closer toward her, fearful she might collapse. "Spirits possess only so much attachment to our world once their bodies die away," Maggie said in a still quiet voice.

"Has he gone to Heaven?" Mrs. Cutler asked, still weeping softly.

"His spirit has moved on from here and to the next life, yes. I wouldn't encourage trying to contact him again. It could interrupt the journey if we were to pull him back," Maggie explained.

Though she had given this comfort many times, she was no more sure that it was true than the first time she had said it. From the beginning, it was no more than a kind explanation, a merciful opportunity for the grieving to move on.

"We cannot thank you enough," Dr. Cutler said, his steady voice now filled with emotion.

"He answered your question to me before it was over," Maggie said, standing as her strength slowly returned.

"Yes?" Dr. Cutler asked.

"You are a physician?"

"I am a doctor, like my father," he confirmed with a nod.

"Your son told me he wanted to be a soldier like you. Have you seen combat?" Maggie asked.

"Why, no, but I served in my youth as an army doctor," Dr. Cutler explained.

"Paulie loved his little soldier men. He always would have battles with them, all across the floor," Mrs. Cutler said.

"It seems you were quite the influence," Maggie encouraged.

"You have our deepest gratitude, Ms. Barlow," he said, nearly to tears as he handed her the payment and shook her hand in accentuation. "This doesn't feel like enough."

"The best thanks is to spread the word. As a doctor, you must come across many families in tragedy," Maggie suggested as she opened the door.

Maggie said her farewells to the Cutlers as they climbed down the stairs and out to the busy street, locked in quiet conversation. Once they were out of sight, Maggie followed them down but instead turned toward the door marked 320 and entered the apartment.

The wood paneled sitting room was warm and welcoming with a hearty fire beneath the mantle. Before it, two armchairs faced a rose colored settee. It was a comfortable space, even if the furnishings were a bit dated. She had made do, decorating the walls with choice pieces of art, and the housekeeper always kept fresh flowers in her favorite vase. Just beyond was the spacious dining room, which was more for show than honest practicality. The apartment was not entirely her own. In reality, it was held under her brother's name, but their parents would not have funded such a comfortable arrangement had she not been staying there as well.

"Isn't it a bit early to be waking the dead?" Jonathan said, face hidden behind his newspaper as he sat in his customary seat in the armchair by the fire.

"Shouldn't you be out counting other people's money?" Maggie retorted.

"Actually, no," he said, setting down the paper with care. Her brother was tall and bore a generally clean cut appearance. As usual, his suit was freshly laundered, and his light brown hair was well groomed. His long nose and narrow lips were the spitting image of their father, who at a younger age was likely as handsome. Though Maggie would always see him as a gangly twelve year old who read too much and had an unnatural fear of garden toads. "Do you have any more appointments today?"

"No," Maggie said, stretching out comfortably on the settee.

"Well, I happen to have dinner plans," he said matter of factly. "I've been talking with Ms. Camila Huddleston. Her father owns several textile factories, one here in the city. She's accepted my invitation for dinner here tonight."

"Is that how men talk about me?" Maggie mused. "Yes, her name is Margaret Ward. Her father owns half the railroad from here to California. I hear his race horses do quite well on the Kentucky circuit."

Though Margaret Ward was her birth name, only her parents called her that. To everyone else, she was Maggie. Maggie Barlow, her alias, had been created as a pseudonym for her professional use, mainly for the purpose of hiding from her parents that she was not in fact scouring the city in search of a suitable husband, but was a moderately successful medium running seances out of her brother's old office space.

"That's how they would if you actually met anyone," he teased. Maggie rolled her eyes as they shared a bout of laughter before his demeanor returned to that of the young, accomplished banker. "I want to impress Camila. So there will be no talk of your business, understood?"

"Well, what if she asks?" Maggie questioned.

"What if she asks if you run a side business of fooling poor people into thinking they are speaking with the great beyond?" he joked.

"Fine," Maggie surrendered.

Jonathan held no belief in the work she did in her peculiar parlor. Having himself installed the device that caused the table's arrow to spin at her behest, Maggie could not fault him for having little faith in her work. What he could not understand was that her clients came to her parlor for spectacle. The pageantry was as necessary as the gifts she truly possessed. What was real and what was show, sometimes the line was blurred even to herself. How could one separate imagination from genuine imperceptible ability?

What she knew for certain was that were she not his sister, he would not indulge the nonsense at all. Yet Jonathan had been in the business of indulging her since they were children. Its effect on him was so powerful that lying to their parents to cover her admittedly unusual venture had seemed only a natural courtesy.

CHAPTER

2

MRS. DOYLE'S GINGER hair was in an unusual state of disarray as she finally pulled the game pie from the oven and set it on the counter with a satisfied sigh. Many strands had fallen loose from her familiar bun as she had spent the afternoon preparing for Jonathan's dinner guest. It had been short notice to change the simple meal she had planned to a formal dinner, but she was proud of what she had been able to put together nonetheless. The housekeeper sat down heavily in one of the kitchen chairs, swiping a stray recipe magazine from the counter and fanning herself. If this kept up, they would need to hire a proper cook, Mrs. Doyle thought to herself, quite unaware that Maggie was lurking in the doorway.

Maggie announced herself, clearing her throat primly.

"Sweet Heavens!" Mrs. Doyle exclaimed, nearly falling from her chair.

"Just checking in," Maggie said pleasantly, smiling to herself.

"Everything will be ready when Ms. Huddleston arrives," Mrs. Doyle said, eyeing her reproachfully.

Ever since Mrs. Doyle had discovered her strange occupation, she was utterly convinced that Maggie had made some unsavory deal with the devil. Though she was an excellent cook and dutiful maid, she refused to enter or clean the upstairs parlor lest she jeopardise her immortal soul. Despite her opposition to cleaning the room, Maggie had often happened upon crucifixes and saintly figures scattered around the parlor. One such discovery occurred in the middle of a sitting when a planted crucifix fell from the curtains, striking a gentleman on the head and causing quite the fright.

Maggie hovered over the game pie, her proximity to the culinary work clearly setting the poor housekeeper on edge. It was a handsome creation with little dough leaves and flowers baked into the crust. Knowing Mrs. Doyle's cooking, it would be delicious on the inside as well. Hopefully, Ms. Huddleston wouldn't begrudge them too much for being a little old fashioned.

"It smells positively sinful!" Maggie said, taking in a deep breath through her nose before leaving Mrs. Doyle's cool stare and the kitchen behind to join Jonathan in the sitting room.

"Is everything ready?" he asked, half dressed and mildly frantic.

"Everything but you," Maggie said as he fumbled with his tie.

"Oh, let me fix it. You better not spoil this tonight because I'm getting tired of taking care of you."

"I could say the same to you," he countered.

"Do you think she'll be here soon?" Maggie asked.

Jonathan reached for the watch kept faithfully in his pocket. However, he had no time to answer her before the doorbell tolled for them. The color flushed from his face as if the reaper itself had come to call. Maggie ignored his gaping jaw and finished her adjustments to his tie.

"I'll get the door," Maggie said, adding sharply, "Tuck in your shirt!"

Maggie went out into the hall, leaving Jonathan to dance madly, trying to fix his appearance. Through the glazed window, Maggie could see a woman's slight silhouette. She answered the door with a smile. The woman looked up at her, expression polite yet obviously confused.

Camila was dressed expensively. It was no doubt that her father's textile factories were profitable, to say the least. However, even without her exquisite fashions, she was an attractive young woman. Her complexion was a tanned olive. Her deep brown eyes were shrouded beneath enviably dark lashes. She had pinned her wavy black hair perfectly around a delicate hat. Though her demeanor was bright and cheerful and at first glance appeared rather carefree, Maggie sensed more beneath her innocuous exterior.

"I'm sorry, I must have the wrong address," she apologised.

"You are Camila?" Maggie asked.

"Yes?" she said, peeking around the corner. "Is Johnathan here?"

As if to answer her question, Jonathan came into the hall to greet her.

"Camila, how wonderful to see you. Please excuse my sister," he said cordially, welcoming her inside the apartment.

"Maggie," she introduced herself, trying heroically not to roll her eyes.

"A pleasure," Camila said, her smile the picture of charm. "What a lovely apartment," she commented, taking a special interest in one of Maggie's favorite pieces of art. "Is it just the two of you?"

"Yes. It's all the room we need," Jonathan said, taking her heavy woolen coat. At first glance, Maggie had not considered her to be particularly short of stature, but seeing her petite figure beside her brother's tall bodied frame accentuated them both to the extremes. It seemed as though there must be at least a foot of difference between them.

From the kitchen, Mrs. Doyle rang the dinner bell.

"Care for some supper?" he asked, reaching his arm out to her.

Camila accepted with a smile, and Maggie followed them to the dining room. Though the table had seating for six, she could not recall a time it had ever been filled. The excessive size was merely a formality for company. In fact, Jonathan and Maggie hardly took meals together at all since he was so fond of eating in his study while buried in work. Maggie however would eat throughout the day, between her appointments, as the whim struck her.

As the meal was served, Maggie ate her portions quietly as Jonathan and Camila talked amongst themselves. She had a freely gay air and laughed often at his stories. Her questions were intelligent and commentary insightful. It was a strange thing that someone like Camila would find her brother as charming as she did. Though, Maggie would admit that she was likely the worst judge of her brother's desirability since she had seen him in so many compromising situations as a child.

"So, Camila." Maggie began as Mrs. Doyle made her way around the table, serving the final course of game pie. "How did you meet my brother?"

"Well, Jonathan was a member of the firm which advises my father's investments."

"I still am," Jonathan added.

"I don't visit my father too often at his offices, but when I did, I was fortunate enough to make your brother's acquaintance."

"I consider myself the lucky one that you accepted my invitation," Jonathan said with a small smile.

"It was a pleasure, really," Camila smiled back.

"And what is it you do, Camila?" Maggie asked, needing some reprieve from the nauseating display of niceties.

Jonathan shot her a look at the impertinent question but softened before Camila could see his displeasure.

"Well, I am a member of the United Methodist Women, and I teach English twice a week at the community house," Camila said. "I've thought very much about going to university for a teaching certificate. What about yourself?"

"Maggie is a student," Jonathan lied before Maggie could answer.

"What are you studying?"

"Yes, I'm studying to be an accountant, like my dear brother," Maggie began as she stabbed at a piece of meat, unable to help herself. Jonathan's face went pale. "In truth, I don't think there is any nobler profession."

"Certainly, teaching English to the illiterate is a far more virtuous endeavour," Jonathan said, shooting another polite smile across the table.

"As a matter of fact, that is true," Maggie began. "I'm sure there are many professions that instill more good into the world than counting other people's money for them. Perhaps I should think of a change in career."

"You know, as I was taking a car here, I told the driver the address. It seemed terribly familiar," Camila said diplomatically. "How long have you lived here?"

"Only two years now, I suppose," Jonathan said, not looking up from his plate.

"I had thought it possible that I once visited the previous tenant, but your home does not seem familiar at all," Camila wondered.

"Well, there are several offices hosted on this street," Maggie prompted, receiving a kick from under the table. "You may be remembering one of them. There's a physician, the lawyer, the tailor across the street."

"I've remembered!" Camila announced excitedly. "Haven't you a medium on this street? One of those spiritualists who hold the sittings?"

"No, I don't think-" Jonathan began, between coughs as he nearly choked on his pie.

"I'm certain I remember from the advertisement, a medium at 321 Warren Street," Camila was quiet for a moment. "But isn't that your address?"

"Of course not," Jonathan dismissed. "We are at 320 Warren Street. 321 is upstairs."

"I only remember so clearly, because the ladies and I were looking for women of the community for a suffrage rally this next Saturday, and I believe that your upstairs medium was on my list to reach out to. Isn't that exciting?" Camila asked.

"I couldn't say," Jonathan admitted, defeated.

"Do you think she would be interested?" Camila asked. "What was her name again?"

"I'm not sure. We've never met her," Jonathan said, looking to Maggie in distress.

"You've never met her, and she lives just upstairs?"

"I believe you might be confused about the address, or perhaps it was misprinted," Jonathan lied.

"Oh, for goodness sake, Jonathan, just tell her the truth," Maggie said, unable to endure his feeble deflections any longer.

Camila eyed him expectantly. Jonathan squirmed for a moment under the weight of their gaze before giving in.

"The medium does work upstairs," Jonathan said.

"Why is that such a confession?" Camila asked, glancing between them. "There must be more. Have you had some affair with this woman?"

"Heavens, no!" Jonathan exclaimed. "It's Maggie."

Camila looked to Maggie in amazement as Maggie looked to Jonathan in equal surprise for actually telling their guest the honest truth. Meanwhile, Jonathan looked down sadly at his plate with childish disappointment as if she had once again broken one of his toys.

"Is that true?"

"Yes," Maggie admitted.

"Could I see upstairs?" Camila asked quite excitedly.

Maggie glanced apprehensively at Jonathan, looking for some glimmer of direction, but he just gazed back blankly in bewilderment at the whole ordeal. "I suppose it couldn't hurt."

"Wonderful," she said, folding her napkin and placing it on her plate as she stood.

"But... Dinner?" Jonathan mumbled, but Camila hadn't heard him.

Camila followed Maggie upstairs, Jonathan begrudgingly behind them. Maggie unlocked the parlor and lit the lamps. Camila entered, looking at every oddity and detail with wonder.

"How macabre," she said, looking at the trio of crows staring down at them from the wardrobe.

"I shot them in my youth with my father," Jonathan said.

"Is that so?" Camila asked. "Sweet of you to lend them. They do add a mystery to the room. Can I ask the purpose of the strapped chair?"

"That chair is for me," Maggie answered. "It reassures patrons that I'm not using tricks or cons."

"Is it frightening?" Camila asked, looking back at Jonathan. "Surely you've sat in many times."

"No, actually, I haven't," Jonathan said.

"It is getting rather dark," Camila said, pulling back the thick curtains.

"Perhaps I should call you a cab," Jonathan suggested.

"But isn't now the perfect time?"

"Whatever for?"

"A sitting, of course," Camila said with a wide smile.

"I'm not sure that..."

"You aren't afraid, are you?" she asked playfully.

"Of course not..." Jonathan said, looking to Maggie desperately.

"Well then, why not?"

"I guess, we could..." he said slowly.

"So what do we do?" Camila asked, turning her attention to Maggie.

"Well, why don't you take a seat at the table," Maggie said, sitting in her own chair. "I'll do something simple. I won't be needing the restraints."

Camila took a seat as Jonathan sulked at her side. Maggie began to extend that invisible sense. There was a strangeness about her brother's presence here, like a colliding of lives, Margaret and Maggie forced into the same room. Still, she was able to reach that familiar whispering mist.

"Is there anyone in particular you wish to speak with?" Maggie asked.

Camila shook her head. "I haven't lost anyone in a great while."

"Are you certain?" Maggie asked. "I feel a presence that moves with you, wishing to speak." A voice was becoming clearer, approaching her freely.

"What sort of spirit?" Camila asked.

"She is young, a child. You were her teacher," Maggie sensed.

"I teach adults, not children," Camila said, brow furrowed.

"Maggie, come let's-" Jonathan began.

"I hear her!" Maggie exclaimed. "I hear her speaking in another tongue. Bring me a paper."

Camila rushed to get paper and a pen from atop the old sewing table, ignoring Jonathan's silent protest and putting it before her. Maggie shut her pale green eyes and began to write as the girl's words filled her mind.

"This is German!" Camila exclaimed.

The voice was so clear, as if the words were being whispered right into her ear. She continued to scribble without thought, and as the connection grew, the words began to pour from Maggie's mouth.

"Zu krank. Keine Medizin. Gehen nicht in die Schule. Kann nicht zur Arbeit gehen."

"She talks of a sickness," Camila translated. "About how she cannot leave the house. What is your name? Wer bist du?"

Maggie took the pen and in dark letters wrote ELSIE SCHNEIDER.

"I knew her. Her mother brought her along every week until a month ago. She's dead?" Camila said tearfully, gloved hands coming to cover her mouth.

"Maggie, isn't this enough?" Jonathan said, agitated.

"No, ask her what she wants," Camila pleaded.

"She has a request," Maggie said, scribbling on the paper absently as she spoke. A picture was in her mind forming so clearly. "The Puppe, the doll. She wants the doll in the blue dress. Her father made it. She wants to be put to rest with it."

"Tell her I will find her mother and tell her about the doll," Camila said.

Maggie let out a deep sigh and rubbed her forehead as the spirit left her. Her body felt weak, cold, as she looked down at her scribblings to see the sketching of a porcelain doll that she had never truly seen, like a drawing of a dream.

"Remarkable," Camila said, taking the sketch. "As if you drew it from life. I remember her with this now, always on her arm."

"How did you do it?" Jonathan asked, looking at the drawing.

Maggie said nothing. She had never minded her brother's skepticism, but now that he had seen her practices with his own eyes, he no longer doubted her absently. He wanted to comfort himself by proving her a fraud.

"You must have met this child before, seen her with Camila," Jonathan accused. "How are we to know that the girl is even dead?"

"Jonathan, leave her alone. What she can do is incredible," Camila scolded.

Maggie's gaze switched from her brother to Camila as she defended her.

"Can't you see it's a trick?" Jonathan said. "Everything she has done could easily be play acted if she had only met the child and asked her about her doll."

"You think your sister followed me before this evening for the purpose of tricking me up here and making a fool of me with information about a little girl's death?" Camila laughed at the implausibility of it all. "Had you even told her my name before today?"

"She could have seen you while I was working," Jonathan posed weakly.

"Honestly, are you so stubborn not to believe?" Camila said harshly as she stood. "Maggie, you are truly gifted, and I hope you don't let him tell you any different. Please join us for the rally next Saturday. We would all love to have you," Camila said, heading for the door. "Good evening, Jonathan."

Maggie watched mutely as Jonathan hurried after her.

He was gone for quite some time. When he finally returned, Maggie was resting by the fire in the sitting room.

"Are you quite satisfied now?" Jonathan demanded, looking rather tired.

"I can't think what for," Maggie said.

"I'll be struck if Camila ever speaks to me again. Heaven hope I still have a job with her father."

"I can't imagine how you would think that is my doing!" Maggie rebutted. "You're the one who upset her!"

"You turned her against me!" His finger jabbed out at her at his accusation. "It's always the same. Why does it always have to be about you? Why can it never just be a quiet dinner?"

"I'm sorry that I'm such an embarrassment!" she snapped, standing from her seat.

"All I want is to make a life, for Heaven's sake, maybe even court someone. Why can't you?"

"Because this is what I want!"

"This is what you want?" he laughed angrily, waving his arms in exclamation. "You want to make me miserable forever while you run some mad sideshow out of my office? That's it! You are actively trying to chase off other women to keep things the way they are!"

"You egocentric ass!" Maggie exclaimed.

Jonathan rested his hands on his hips. "I just don't see why you have to do all of this."

"I'm not trying to keep you from finding someone. I like Camila. But I don't want that for me now. I like my life as it is."

There was a pause, and Jonathan let out a deep sigh.

"I'm sorry," Maggie apologised in a moment of rare penitence. "I do want your happiness."

"I'll write Camila tonight and see if there's a chance she'll see me again,"

"I think she really is fond of you," Maggie added. "Just make sure you apologise."

Jonathan huffed a great breath out again and rubbed the ridge of his nose. "I'm going to die alone, an old bachelor with a circus in my office."

"Let's just hope she writes you back then," Maggie said, smiling wryly as she went off to bed.

CHAPTER

3

MAGGIE SAT ON THE CUSHIONED stool before her vanity, examining her work. Though she possessed a naturally fair complexion, Maggie brushed the white powder over her face once more, looking to achieve the theatrical paleness which, in the dim light of her parlor, gave an ethereal appearance. While in finishing school, Maggie had longed to be an actress. She had appeared in more than one of her school's productions, and though her parents would never have approved of her use of cosmetics, she had studied their tricks. They served her now in delivering the proper atmosphere to her sittings.

"Maggie, a caller for you," Jonathan called from the front of the house.

Maggie checked the time on the mantelpiece clock, just after three in the afternoon. Her quarter to four appointment was rather early to be arriving. Maggie smoothed her hand over her plum skirts and adjusted her delicate golden necklace before she stood. As she made her way down the hall, Maggie began to fear that this may be another unannounced suitor sent to her by their parents. When she set eyes on the man in the tan suit waiting in their sitting room, she knew immediately that her fears had been wrong. He sported black wire spectacles and a leather doctor's style bag at his side. His tan cotton suit, though not ill fitting, was not hand tailored or pressed. He was clearly not from money or the high station that her parents would normally parade before her.

"Ms. Barlow, I presume?" the bespectacled stranger asked. His brown hair was combed neatly over his round features.

"I am at a disadvantage," Maggie said, now entirely unsure who this man could possibly be to address her by her pseudonym. "You know my name, and I can't seem to recall yours."

"You don't know this man?" Jonathan asked, seated in the armchair behind her. "When he asked for you, I thought he was here on appointment."

"As I said," he explained, flustered to clarify the situation. "You have me quite mistaken. I am here for Ms. Barlow, but not for a personal visit. I am Walter Davies with the ASPR."

"What, may I ask, is the nature of your organization?" Jonathan asked.

"Excuse me," Walter said, clearing his throat to explain. "The American Society for Psychical Research has sent me here to evaluate Ms. Barlow and her claims as a medium, in the hope, if her claims are substantiated, to research her talents in the name of science."

"Science," Jonathan scoffed, choking on his tea. "Are you with the government?" he asked as if it were the most ludicrous thing he could have imagined.

"Indeed I am," Walter said pointedly, handing him a business card from his pocket.

Jonathan took it and began to examine the card as if it were written in some cryptic dialect.

"Please excuse my brother," Maggie said, sweeping between the two. "He is a skeptic. If you wish, I have an appointment at quarter to four. You are welcome to observe."

Walter nodded simply. "I would like to see your sitting parlor. I have some equipment that needs to be put in place before we begin."

"Of course, just this way," Maggie instructed. "Care to join us?" Maggie asked Jonathan as he finally looked up from the card.

"You two enjoy yourselves. I'll send your appointment upstairs," Jonathan said, sitting back in his chair and unfolding the paper. "If he starts experimenting on you, just scream and I'll loose the dogs."

Maggie rolled her eyes as she walked up the narrow stairs and unlocked the parlor, leading Walter inside. He was quiet for several moments, taking in the many curious details.

"Now, do such decorations serve a technical purpose, or are they merely for ambiance?" Walter asked, eyeing her many curios and trinkets.

"I find clients expect a certain unusual atmosphere which only a bout of such theatricality can provide," Maggie explained. "There are however tools here as well."

She took a single stick of incense from the vase where she kept them and handed it to Walter who eyed it curiously. The sharp smell of the spices filled her senses instantly and lingered in the air.

"This is called incense. I buy it from a small oriental shop. They have burned it for centuries in the East for its calming effects."

"Do these help you channel the spirits?" he asked.

"I use them on occasions when I must have an especially potent connection. Usually in circumstances where a specific answer must be found."

"I have heard of a particularly impressive account of how you assisted an heir to find his missing fortune," Walter said, taking a seat.

"Yes, he came to me after his mother's death. His parents had hidden the family's money to keep it from his gambling habits. Unfortunately, the mother died unexpectedly, and she was the last one who knew where the money had been hidden. The money was found in a certain French bank under a false name."

"You were able to name the bank and the name under which the account had been placed?"

"Granted, such accuracy is not always possible," Maggie explained rather proudly. "Sometimes connections are weak or the spirits uncooperative."

"Uncooperative?" Walter questioned.

"Well, they are people, or they were. Sometimes they aren't in the mood to talk. One also must filter at times. Sometimes the dead have unkind sentiments for those they leave behind. Better sometimes to say nothing than to bring up buried arguments."

"Let's hope your next client is more obligating. Are you aware of the nature of his business?"

"I believe he wrote that he has recently lost his wife," Maggie answered.

"I'm sure he'll be arriving soon. Allow me to set up a few instruments."

"Please," Maggie invited, "anything you need."

Walter pulled a contraption from his bag and set it on the table. Two copper poles about a foot in length protruded from the supporting structure. Maggie inspected the device, hoping to discover its purpose.

"This here can detect the presence of spiritual activity in a room through the way it manipulates the electrical currents between the conducting rods," Walter explained.

"Electricity," Maggie echoed.

"Let me show you," he elected eagerly. Walter turned the knob, and a white arch of energy formed between the rods moving constantly but never losing its connection to the copper poles.

"Is that safe?" Maggie asked.

"Perfectly," Walter reassured. "You can even touch it if you wish."

Maggie put out her hand slowly, and to her surprise, the arch reached for her and nipped her finger.

"It feels like I've been stung by a bee!" Maggie gasped, watching the arch return to its former shape.

"I have the voltage set very low. A higher setting could send a man clear across the room."

"Fascinating, truly, but how does it detect the spirits?"

"You see how it was drawn to your finger?" Walter asked, thoroughly enjoying her keen interest. "We believe that ghosts have the same effect, only stronger. A spirit's presence will agitate and attract the current."

"Amazing," Maggie laughed.

"The science is an adaptation of Tesla's work. I'm sure you'll recognise this next piece," Walter said, retrieving a large thermometer from his bag.

"Next you'll tell me that spirits control the weather," Maggie joked.

"Not the weather, exactly, but we are led to believe that a ghost's presence lowers the temperature of the room significantly during contact."

Maggie found herself speechless for a moment. "When I make a connection," she explained slowly, "I feel a chill in my own body. The closer I become to the spirit, the colder it feels. But it is different from a winter's chill. How so is difficult to explain."

Walter pulled out a small book and began recording notes. "If you don't mind, that is a simply fascinating detail. In the future, perhaps I could monitor your own body temperature at the time of connection, as you call it."

Before Maggie could answer, a dark haired man with a somber expression came to stand in the doorway. The atmosphere became sobered as he entered hesitantly. He was quite tall and broad shouldered beneath his neatly tailored coat. Between the black of his overcoat and his dark, oiled hair, it was as if he were a walking shadow unto himself. Though he carried himself with an equally solemn demeanor, Maggie found herself drawn to him. His jaw was squared beneath prominent cheekbones. Heavy brows shadowed his brown eyes, giving them a bewitchingly dark appearance as if one could fall right in if not careful.

"Are you Ms. Barlow?" he asked with a low, rolling voice.

Maggie caught herself gaping unprofessionally and collected herself. "Yes, of course, come in, Mr. Blackbourne," she greeted graciously.

"Charles, please. I must apologise if you are still with another client," Charles began, eyes shifting to Walter.

36

"No, we are more than ready for you. This here is Mr. Walter Davies, and he is with the, forgive me if I remember this falsely, American Society of Psychical Research," Maggie introduced.

"Well said," Walter commented as he shook the client's hand. "And you are, sir?"

"Forgive me. I am Charles Blackbourne."

"Of the Abbott and Blackbourne firm?" Walter asked.

"Yes, I've been a partner there since my uncle's retirement."

"I hope you don't mind if I sit in, for research purposes, of course," Walter asked politely.

"I'm sure that will be quite alright," Charles said. He shed his long overcoat and deposited it on the hanger by the door.

"Very good then. Mr. Blackbourne, if you would have a seat while Mr. Davies finishes his preparations," Maggie said, offering him a chair.

Charles took his seat slowly, still taking in his surroundings. Maggie sat in her chair beside him, feeling conscious of her every movement, as Walter dug further into his bag.

"Now, Mr. Blackbourne, in your letter, I believe you wrote that you are trying to contact your wife?" Maggie asked.

"If it is possible, yes."

"Can you tell me about her?"

"Well, um," Mr. Blackbourne rubbed his hands together, struggling to find where to begin. "We were married for two years, well, very nearly. She passed three months ago. Anne loved music and her garden..." he explained. "She was in her garden when she-

37

She fell from the ladder. The doctor said she suffered a broken neck. They said it was a sudden death."

"I am very sorry for your loss," Maggie said.

He paused for a moment, his dark eyes lingering on her. "I am not usually the sort to believe in such business."

"I understand."

He exhaled a weight from his shoulders. "I only thought that if- Well... if she wished to speak- If such a thing were possible..."

"You would like me to reach out to her, see if she has a message for you?"

He sat pondering for a moment before he answered her with a simple "Yes."

"Mr. Davies, are you ready to begin?"

"Of course. If you wouldn't mind, I should like to record our sitting for posterity."

"I have no contest to the idea," Maggie answered.

"Mr. Blackbourne?" Walter asked.

"Yes, of course," Charles dismissed.

"Before you begin recording, would you be so kind as to fasten the restraints, Mr. Davies?" Maggie asked.

"Whatever for?" Charles asked.

"For my own safety and your peace of mind," Maggie replied simply.

Walter bound her feet and then her wrists with clinical focus.

"May we begin?" Walter asked as he stood.

"Please," Maggie answered, and Walter put the needle to the record.

"Hello, the date is October 27th, 1916. I, Walter Davies of the ASPR, am here with prospective medium Maggie Barlow and her client who has sought Ms. Barlow's assistance in contacting the deceased, his wife."

The trio sat in silence for a moment as they waited, senses peaked for signs of a presence besides their own. Maggie opened her mind with an unusual intent. A hidden desire had surfaced itself with Mr. Davies' arrival, to prove that her gift was genuine, measurable, and thus undeniable.

"Join hands with me," Maggie instructed.

As Mr. Blackbourne's palm came against her own, any hint of that frigid abyss faded from her as his warmth overcame her senses. The shock overrode her for only a moment before she exhaled profoundly and reigned in her traitorous mind.

"Mrs. Blackbourne, we are here to listen to you. Speak to us if you can hear me." Maggie said into the darkness of the room.

They sat anxiously, waiting. Around them, she felt only the ordinary distant hum of a thousand indistinguishable voices. No pull, no pronounced, lingering presence. Maggie thought to use her tricks as she would ordinarily rely on if she did not sense an immediate presence. However, she was far too eager to impress her present company to default to parlor tricks.

"Mr. Blackbourne, perhaps you could try calling your wife by name. Your familiar voice may draw her to us."

"Anne," Charles called hesitantly. "Anne, darling. Can you speak to us?"

At his plea, Mr. Walter's electric device began to surge. The veil which had been dormant on the edges of her perception suddenly gripped her mind, pulling her as far as she had ever dared venture before.

"She's with us," Maggie said through a shuddering breath. Never had she encountered a connection so forceful, powerful enough to pull her deeper into the darkness rather than lead. Maggie forced herself to calm as the chill spread down her back. She would not release the hold. "Anne, speak to us and I will hear you."

"My God!" Charles exclaimed, spinning in his chair. "I've felt a hand just now on my shoulder."

"Her connection is strong. She-" Again, she felt the overwhelming pull, plunging her into the icy darkness. Far away, her body trembled uncontrollably.

"Ms. Barlow, are you alright?" Walter asked, feeling her brow.

"Dear god," Charles asked. "Must we call a doctor?"

"I'm alright," Maggie said, teeth chattering.

"Tell us, what do you see?" Walter asked.

"I see-" Maggie began, the men hanging on her every word as she described the vision playing through her mind. It was dull as a distant memory but as real as any of her own. "I see the garden from her eyes. She is standing on a ladder, trimming with her shears. She is happy. She's woken early and has something planned."

"She had received a letter that her brother would be-" Charles said.

"Something is happening!" Maggie gasped as a force pulled her backward. A shot of icy terror gripped the memory and ran through her own body. "She's begun to fall. Someone has pulled her back. Her dress is torn. She knows that someone has done this to her. Someone caused her to fall! Someone is to blame."

"What do you mean?" Charles protested. "Her death was an accident."

"It was murder," Maggie said, voice nothing but frantic pants as the cold began to burn her skin in icy rage. "She tells me. Someone has caused her to fall. She wishes to cry out, but the fall is too short. It plays through her mind. Murder, murder, murder."

"Enough!" Charles demanded, his warm hand ripped from her own as he stood.

All at once, Maggie felt herself falling back through the veil, to the light of the parlor and the warmth of her own body. The collision brought a wave of dizzy nausea, and Maggie could not help but clench her eyes shut against it.

"My wife was not murdered," Charles said, straightening his suit coat sharply. "This is some wretched trick. What manner of con would shock the grieving with such a scandal for their own profit? I will not have you speak of my wife!"

"Mr. Blackbourne, please," Maggie pleaded, still feeling weakened as Walter relieved her restraints. "Your wife is speaking to you. Please listen! Someone caused her to fall, her dress was torn, it-"

"I will not listen to any more of this," Charles said, fetching his hat and storming down the stairs.

Maggie let out a deep sigh, far too weak to chase after the man and confident he wouldn't listen to her even if she did.

"Are you alright?" Walter asked after a moment.

"I will be," Maggie said, trying and failing to stand.

"Please rest if you must," Walter urged her.

"Thank you," Maggie said, forehead resting on her fingers. A swelling headache was coming over her, followed at the heels by another bout of chilled nausea. What she would not give for a hot cup of tea, maybe even a steaming bath.

"Is it always so taxing on your person?"

She shook her head. "Her spirit was more forceful than I have experienced. I must apologise. I have never had this happen before."

"Mr. Blackbourne's response was regrettable but understandable given the sensitive nature of the revelation," Walter said, powering off his instruments and examining them. "However, what I observed today was unlike anything I have witnessed. Both of my devices recorded substantial activity."

"Well, I'm very glad you got the results you were hoping for," Maggie said pointedly.

"I'm sure this will benefit your business as well when I publish you as a credible psychic in the journal."

"Will you really?" Maggie asked, perking up slightly.

"I believe you have the true gift," Walter said, packing his things into his bag. "You are just the sort that our organization looks for. We hope one day to really seek out and understand individuals like yourself. Maybe one day we can reverse the years of stigma and move forward. Today is the day of science after all."

CHAPTER

4

MAGGIE SWEPT INTO THE sitting room, pulling on her thick woolen suit coat. The chill was setting in early this year, and Maggie had no tolerance for it. It matched her blue skirt, with bronze embroidery decorating the hem and the sleeves. The accompanying hat mirrored the color with long accenting pheasant feathers.

"Do you have an appointment?" Jonathan asked as he straightened his tie in the mirror above the mantelpiece.

"The suffrage rally is this morning," Maggie answered, humoring him as she searched for her favorite gloves.

She knew too well that Jonathan had been waiting in the sitting room for some twenty minutes, putting him past his precise departure time for his work at the bank, to ambush her with this question which he very well knew the answer to.

"Oh, would that be the same as Camila mentioned at dinner the other night?" he said in a mock casual voice, still fixated on his reflection.

"Yes," Maggie said, flexing her fingers into her gloves.

Jonathan finally turned to look at her as she went to the door, his expression lost for words, yet she could see his request burning behind his lips.

"She still hasn't written you?"

"I've always said the post system in this city was faulty," he said, fidgeting with his watch chain before catching the nervous gesture and righting himself.

"Shall I ask her about you? See if she's meant to write?" Maggie suggested, sparing him finally.

"I would appreciate it," Jonathan said, his demeanor shifting at once as he grabbed his case. "We've been terribly busy at the bank, and I'm very late. I'll see you for dinner," he said, opening the door for her and following her out.

Maggie rolled her eyes at her brother's childish charade. As if he fooled her; for all his talk of business and lofty manners, he was still her childhood companion underneath. Someone who she much preferred to the pompous stranger he had become ever since he went off to the academy. She had only been nine years old then and frightfully bored, cooped up with some nanny or another in the country estate. It hadn't mattered how much she missed him though because he had returned from break eager to impress their father with the newfound manners of a gentleman, an endeavour that had never truly ended to that day.

Across the city, the suffrage rally was being held in the reception rooms at a stylish hotel downtown. A large crystal chandelier hung from the center of the lobby. As she entered, a cleanly dressed valet showed her to the ballroom through the flowing crowd of hotel guests and attendees gathered for the same event. They talked in huddled masses clad in ribbons and sashes, whispering about the cause and the day's speakers as well as many unrelated topics of gossip and intrigue.

The ballroom was filled with many round tables decorated with swelling floral arrangements. The gilded mirrors on the walls reflected the pastel dresses of the ladies and the bouquets making the room seem like an endless garden of color. Tea and delicate cakes made their way between the tables on small trolleys.

The women were engaged in a multitude of conversations creating a lively buzz throughout the room. Maggie tucked a stray curl behind her ear as she scanned the crowd. She recognised a few faces from previous introductions but nothing more. Most were fashionable women of some means, but only a few bore the marks of true fortune. Yet, to her distress, Maggie could find no sign of the soul who had invited her.

"Is there a problem, miss?" the valet asked.

"No, no, thank you," Maggie said, dismissing him and stepping into the ballroom.

"Oh, excuse me!" a woman called from inside the doorway.

The small, brown haired woman scurried to her side with a basket of purple and gold ribbons.

"You'll need one of these," the woman said, fastening the pin to her chest.

"Oh, thank you," Maggie said instinctively, still searching for anyone familiar.

"Maggie!" Camila's voice called.

Maggie released a sigh and turned to see Camila standing at a half empty table waving for her to join them. She smiled and waved back to acknowledge she had seen the invitation before making her way to join them.

"This is Ms. Margaret Ward," Camila introduced. "Maggie, this is Charlotte Hobbs, Susan Thorpe, and Pauline Foster."

They exchanged polite hellos as Maggie took a seat at the table. Before each of them was a collection of threads, needles, and an embroidery hoop. The women who had each been focused on their crafts before she entered returned to their work. Pauline and Charlotte were engaged in deep conversation, whispering behind their gloved hands and laughing lightly. Susan however sat beside them, stitching quietly. Her blonde hair was tied up loosely, a few wispy strands falling to her shoulder to touch the lace collar of her blouse.

"We are making prayer squares for our fellow sisters who find themselves under incarceration for the cause," Camila whispered, resuming her work as well. "That's the pattern there." She slid the paper across the table so they could share view of it as Maggie took the piece of fabric already held tight in the hoop and a spool of string. It was a simple pattern of a cross surrounded by flowers and a pair of doves. She went to work on it mindlessly. It had been over a year since she had practiced needlepoint, but it had been so ingrained into her upbringing that the habit returned to her with ease.

"So, Susan," Camila began, "have you found suitable accommodations here in the city?"

"Yes," she said lightly. "My sister and her husband have been kind enough to allow me to stay for a while."

"It is remarkable that your brother-in-law is willing to take on such a burden," Charlotte said mildly. Unlike Susan, Charlotte's build was thicker, her face rounder. Her black hair was tucked neatly in an intricate fashion. She wore a plaid vest over her blouse, which crisscrossed in tones of green. Beside her, Pauline nodded in accentuation. Her brilliant red hat was precariously bordering the line between ostentatious and garish. Though her burgundy tailored coat beneath was enviably stylish.

"Susan's company is hardly a burden," Camila said, almost abrasively. "What is most important is that our dear friend has a safe place to stay and doesn't have to leave us."

Susan smiled weakly, looking down at her work. They were all silent for a time, focusing on their crafts. Maggie was slow to restart any conversation since she was sure she was missing most of a complex story behind Susan's relocation.

It was clear that Camila's opinion was a powerful force here. She was unafraid to defend her friends or to speak plainly. God above, Maggie detested nothing more than banter where no one spoke a word of what they were truly thinking. The longer Maggie spent around Camila, the more endearing she found her. Certainly better than any of the other empty headed girls Jonathan had brought home in the past.

"I think it was right of you to go," Pauline said, catching Susan off guard. "If the world were any way decent, it would be Mr. Thorpe banging down his sister's door for a place to stay." Her stern manner played naturally on her prim features.

"That is the truth," Charlotte agreed fervently. "A man like that..." She seemed too passionate to suggest what a man like that should do and instead directed her attention violently back to her needlepoint.

Maggie almost smirked to see her tone change so quickly on the matter.

"That is why our message of temperance and equality is so important," Camila added sagely. "We cannot stand by to be victims in our own homes."

"And not to mention the children," Charlotte said, shaking her head again.

"I hadn't even thought!" Pauline said, hand grasping her chest. "Those poor dears alone in the house with that man."

Susan stood up. Maggie realised only now that she was very near an episode of tears. "Please excuse me," she breathed almost inaudibly through a tight throat.

She hurried away at a brisk pace. Pauline and Charlotte shared a worried look and promptly followed her from the ballroom, though Maggie was unsure if they would be able to help the situation.

"Some people just do not know when to hold their tongues," Camila said crossly as she continued her work.

"Did she really have to leave her children behind?" Maggie asked quietly.

"She's doing everything she can to bring them with her, but the house is in her husband's name, and without a place to live, it's unlikely the courts will side in her favor. Even if she could find somewhere, the divorce and custody hearings would take months," Camila explained. "I'm nearly certain she'll go back within the week. She can't stand being away from them."

"Surely the police could do something," Maggie said. "If he is hurting her, then-"

Camila shook her head and looked as though about to speak when they were interrupted by the first of the speakers.

"Ladies, your attention please," said a voice through the microphone. A polite hush came over the room as many hurried to their seats. "Our guest speaker, Mrs. Milford, will be talking to us today about the future of the cause and our successes on the congressional front."

Applause carried through the hall as the young woman stepped back, and Mrs. Milford took the stage in a green dress with a high collar. The older woman spoke with eloquent passion as she described the struggles of women, both within the states and abroad, and ultimately the fight for suffrage. Camila's hands seemed to work independently of her mind as she focused completely on every word.

Susan returned with the others with as much dignity as possible for one who had obviously been past the point of consolability only moments before. Maggie did her best not to stare as the others focused their attention on the speaker. It was strange to think of a woman who appeared so near her own age as a mother when Maggie could not think it a possibility for herself. Not that children were repulsive or undesirable to her, in fact it was a fantasy of hers to be a mother, but it was a distant dream for another time in her life.

"So, Maggie, how is your brother?" Camila said, drawing Maggie from her thoughts.

The speaker had stepped down, and applause was had. Maggie realised she had clapped along beyond her conscious knowledge.

"Well, he says things at the bank are going well. He seems content," Maggie said, coyly skirting the true nature of her question.

"I'm glad to hear he is doing well," she said carefully, looking down at her nearly finished work.

"Is that the man you had dinner with the other night?" Charlotte asked.

"Yes, he was," Camila said shortly, sitting up straighter and focusing ever more on her needlework.

"So you must be the medium she was talking about!" Pauline whispered excitedly.

"Yes, she is so talented!" Camila said. She then continued to portray a grand retelling of the seance that the others followed in marveled silence. It all sounded so fantastical from her telling, Maggie felt as though she was speaking about some magnificent stranger.

"Well, when are you seeing him again?" Pauline asked.

Camila pursed her lips.

"Don't tell me you mean not to," Charlotte said, eyes widening hungrily at the prospect of new gossip.

"You seemed so fond of him at our last meeting," Pauline added. "What happened?"

"It was simply a bad match," Camila said shortly.

"He sounded very sweet when you spoke about him," Susan said quietly.

"I thought so," Camila said weakly.

"Has he asked to meet again?" Pauline asked.

"He did write a rather lengthy apology and asked if I would meet him for tea to explain himself," Camila said.

Maggie could see her resolve faltering, and thus she struck. "I can tell you honestly, Camila, that he has been sullen for days. He wouldn't let me out the door this morning unless I promised to speak with you."

"You think he is truly sorry?" Camila asked. "You know him better than anyone. Is that normally his way?"

"My brother," Maggie began, unsure of what exactly she was going to say even as the words began spilling from her mouth. "He was so excited and rather nervous as well to have you for dinner and that's what you saw. He was trying so hard to impress you with a proper meal and conversation. Jonathan gets tied up in himself trying to impress people. You just have to exercise a fair bit of patience with him, and he will be the thoughtful, loyal, and charming man he truly is."

"Oh, you could sell water to the ocean," Camila scoffed. "I'll write him back this afternoon."

Pauline and Charlotte then demanded to hear every detail of their first dinner together. Susan and Maggie listened quietly until it was time to return home. Many of the women from other tables came to exchange goodbyes with Camila. She introduced Maggie to each one of her admirers by name before they went out through the extravagant lobby and onto the street.

They hailed a cab, and the driver helped them inside.

"I'm so happy you came today," Camila said once they were in motion. "It's always nice to have a friend at those sorts of things."

"A friend?" Maggie scoffed. "It seemed like you knew everyone there."

Camila laughed. "I've been with the cause for some years now, and I've lived in the city for longer still. Of course, I have acquaintances. But I feel I can talk more freely with you."

"Well, I'm glad I came as well. It is good to get out of that apartment. It is such a masculine space."

"Well, I rather enjoyed it at dinner," Camila said. "Thank you for talking to me today, about your brother. I can be so stubborn sometimes. I know he is like you said, thoughtful and he means well. When we met at my father's office," Camila recalled, "he was all of those things. He deserves a chance to make amends."

"He'll be so pleased you've changed your mind," Maggie said.

"You know, my dear cousin, Richard, is coming into the city next week. He wrote me yesterday asking if we could meet for dinner. Perhaps you and Jonathan could accompany us?"

"This cousin of yours," Maggie said crisply, "he isn't by any chance available, is he?"

"In fact, he is!" Camila said, her full lips drawn into a wide smile. "He's just finished a tour in Paris as an art consultant to an influential family, but he's back in the country now and plans to stay."

"An art consultant?" Maggie asked, now truly intrigued.

"Yes! I think you two would get on quite well."

"So why is such a catch not already caught, I wonder?" Maggie asked suspiciously.

"Well, that is simple. He's just graduated two years ago from an all men's college and has spent all the time since travelling to establish his career. He hasn't been anywhere long enough to meet anyone suitable until now." She concluded her explanation with a gleeful smile.

"I think you'll find both Jonathan and myself agreeable to the idea," Maggie said conspiratorially.

"Trust me, Maggie. I think you'll like him very much," Camila paused for a moment, looking shy, even nervous. "Just let my letter surprise him, will you?"

"Of course."

CHAPTER

5

IT WAS ONE OF THOSE fortuitous coincidences, which are rare and generally spectacular, that Maggie and Camila shared the same favorite restaurant in Manhattan. This made deciding where to meet pleasantly simple and without conflict. However, it did little to dissuade her brother's nerves as Jonathan spent the entire car ride worrying his watch chain and adjusting his suit. His thin lips moved almost imperceptibly, intently rehearsing some conversation in his mind. Maggie did not disturb him, no matter how silly his manner appeared. She had no doubt that this dinner had been preying on his mind since he had accepted Camila's invitation the week before, as he had spoken of little else since.

As they stepped out onto the street, Maggie pulled her favorite fur coat tighter around herself. The fall breeze was turning quickly to winter's chill, the kind that set into the bones. Jonathan escorted her inside as Maggie quietly enjoyed the many turned heads that followed them. The sensation was even more gratifying when the host offered to take her coat. Beneath, she had worn one of her favorite dinner gowns. It was a scarlet silk dress with black appliques trailing from the bust to the hem of the skirt, which drew behind her in a short train. The bodice was cut to accentuate the curve of her waist in a tasteful, though suggestive manner. With it, Maggie had worn a tightly beaded necklace that hugged the throat and held a sizable garnet stone to sit in the flat of the chest. She caught more than one young man's eyes straying to her figure for a moment or more.

Maggie took in a breath as a wave of satisfaction came over her. Despite herself, she was looking forward to meeting Camila's cousin, Richard. He didn't sound at all like the stuffy bores that her parents found for her. Though Maggie did admit that her imagination had run away with her a bit, having never actually met him to judge for herself.

Jonathan spoke briefly with the host who soon showed them to the table where Camila was waiting for them. Beside her was a young man with brilliant blue eyes. His hair was blonde and curled slightly as Camila's did. Though there were few other similarities between them, Richard's coloring being far fairer. His cheekbones were prominent and rosy, generally giving his face a cheerful demeanor. The pair stood politely to greet them.

"So good of you to join us," Camila said. She had clearly been anticipating this evening as well. The dress she had chosen was a magnificent blue with patterns of gold embroidery which accented

her skin's warm bronze coloring. The neckline was cut to show the extent of her collarbones and the barest hint of her shoulder, where the capped sheer sleeves hung loosely. Maggie saw her brother visibly swallow as she acknowledged him with a nod, pulling himself to his full height. "Richard, this is Mr. Jonathan Ward," Camila introduced. The two exchanged a masculine handshake. "And this is his sister, Margaret."

"Maggie, this is my cousin, Mr. Richard Huddleston."

"Oh, Richard, please," he said as Maggie reached out her hand, and he kissed the back of her glove. Overall, his features were quite pleasing indeed.

"A pleasure to meet you," Maggie said. "Camila spoke of you so fondly."

Richard laughed, his cheeks growing charmingly rosy. "I could say the same of you. My cousin holds you in high esteem."

At last, they found their seats.

"Camila, you are looking very well," Jonathan commented as casually as he could muster.

"I have been quite well," Camila said, looking up from the menu.

Jonathan looked as if he might say something more but balked and began to study the wine list intently.

Camila turned her attention to her cousin. "Richard, tell Margaret about your latest venture. I've told her about your presence in the art world, and she showed a great deal of interest."

"Of course," Richard said, turning to her. "I've just finished helping a Duke in acquiring art for his chateau in France. It was in the most beautiful country. I wish I had not been there on business and could have spent more time exploring. Though I did get the chance to ride with his son through the estate once. It was exquisite, rolling hills of the most fertile vineyards, wildflower fields that stretched like oceans. Of course, the weather was magnificent. It is not hard to imagine how such great art can come from a place of such inspiration. Unfortunately, the conflict in Europe escalated so far that I was forced to return home. Have you been abroad much?"

"Of course," Jonathan said.

"We schooled abroad. Our mother insisted on a proper English education. Though, I haven't been to Paris since I was a little girl," Maggie said.

"France is lovely, to be sure, but I have to say I have a heart for the exotic. I must see India or Africa before I grow too old for adventure."

"I have such fond memories of my childhood in Calcutta," Camila said.

"That does sound exciting!" Maggie agreed.

The waiter came to take their orders for dinner and poured them each a glass of champagne.

"I can only hope that my work takes me there and leaves me enough time to see anything but the insides of expensive mansions and art halls."

"Do they have art halls in Africa?" Maggie wondered, taking a sip of the light bubbling liquid.

"Well, I must explore and find out," Richard said with a laugh.

"Camila, where did you school?" Jonathan asked.

"Here, in the city, at the Finch school," Camila said. "Mother and Father didn't wish to send me too far. We don't have many familial connections in Europe, though we did take a tour of France when I was young."

Jonathan nodded and took a sip of his champagne. Camila had noticeably pushed her own glass farther from her plate, undrunk. Clearly, she took the temperance of her cause seriously.

"All the travel is wonderful, but I do look forward to these next months of peace," Richard said.

"Well, I am happy too," Camila said. "It has been such a pleasure to see you again. It has been such a long time."

"Yes, and I hope to see you often now that I will be in the states," Richard said. "You must come to visit us. I can introduce you to my Elizabeth."

"Who?" Camila asked as Maggie nearly choked.

"Oh, I thought for sure I had mentioned her in one of my letters. She is an old pen pal of mine, one I've been growing rather close to over this past year. We've begun courting again since my return. I am intent to seek an engagement before the year is out."

"Excuse me," Maggie said, standing from the table unceremoniously.

Maggie walked out of the dining room at a brisk and determined pace, eyes becoming wet with anger and embarrassment. The restaurant was hosted by one of the most fashionable hotels in the city. Many were milling about the lobby, others sitting at the hotel bar. She hoped none of them could see the signs of her distress as Maggie cut a course for the lady's room for a few moments of private self indulgence.

Suddenly, a firm hand grabbed her arm. Maggie whirled around, all too surprised to even let out a sound. It was unmistakably Mr. Charles Blackbourne. Though it had been weeks since she had given his reading, she had not forgotten the sharp features of his face nor his dark eyes that looked at her now wide with anger. Something about him was undone, and Maggie found herself paralysed by fright.

"What is this?" he demanded in a threatening hiss, shaking her by the arm. "Have you been following me?"

"Of course not!" Maggie said, finally finding herself over the shock. She ripped herself from his grip and returned a hot glare which might well have been capable of burning small insects.

He glared back at her with agitation, though his rage was fading. It seemed he was again becoming aware of the others milling about the hotel lobby. "Then why are you here?"

"I should say that it is entirely none of your business," Maggie said, eyes narrowed. "But if you must know, I am at dinner with my brother."

His brow raised in evident surprise, taking in her fine dress, the jewel of her necklace. A lady of her standing, a medium. It was a surprise, no doubt.

"Ms. Margaret Ward," Maggie introduced, extending her hand.

Charles took it politely. His lips barely brushed her as his gaze never left her own.

"Please accept my apologies," he said slowly. "You must understand my confusion."

"Your confusion is understandable, but your violence is not," Maggie said, turning away.

"No, wait," he said, taking her arm again, softly this time.

"Are you planning to make a habit of pulling at me whenever you want my attention?" Maggie snapped.

"Please, excuse me," he said.

She watched him closely as he straightened himself, trying to regain his composure.

"I just, perhaps you could..." Charles stumbled, unable to complete his own thought. "Would you join me?" he managed at last, nodding toward the bar. "I could order something for you, to apologise."

She knew that after his outburst, the prudent thing would be to excuse herself from his company immediately. However, few would ever accuse her of being any such thing. There was a disheveled pleading look in his eyes as he asked her to stay which intrigued her.

"You can order me one drink," Maggie said primly.

"I'm not keeping you from anything?" he said. A small measure of relief touched his voice.

"Absolutely not."

"Your brother?"

"He'll be glad of my absence, I'm sure."

Charles nodded and escorted her back to his small table by the bar and offered her a chair.

"Anything I can get for you, sir, miss?" the waiter asked as soon as she was seated.

"I'll have something white," Maggie said. "But nothing French," she added with a sour expression.

"A brandy, please," Charles said with a dismissing nod.

"You seem distressed," Maggie asked in a soft tone when they were alone.

"It is natural for the bereft to be distressed, I've heard."

"If you wish to be coy, I will take my apology and go," Maggie said pointedly.

He eyed her for a moment as the waiter returned and placed the drinks before them.

"I am sorry to have spoken harshly. It was unfair and inexcusable."

"Very well then," Maggie said. She took the wine glass by the stem and moved to stand. His hand caught hers, and her breath hitched. "Mr. Blackbourne," she breathed.

He corrected himself at once, releasing her. "I am sorry, I-Forgive me." His hand combed through his thick black hair. "I find this very difficult, you must understand. Too many things have occurred in these last months..." Charles looked up at her with those dark, pleading eyes. "Things I cannot explain."

"Tell me," Maggie said, lowering her voice. "Perhaps I can help."

His eyes were heavy with contemplation before he nodded and spoke. "When I met with you, the occurrences had already begun. They were not so strange as to be of the paranormal but queer enough to cause my mind to wonder. But after our meeting, what I saw and felt there, I convinced myself it was only a cruel mixture of my own grief and imagination. I knew it was not possible for you to have truly reached her on the other side. It couldn't be..." Charles's eyes went far away as he drew his fingers around his lips. "But in the days of late, there have been happenings in my home that I can no longer ignore. I so wished to believe that it was some odd conspiracy, seeing you here... I wished to believe that you were responsible for it all. But in my rational mind, I know that this is not possible. The only alternative is to trust you. What you say Anne told you, it must be true."

"Mr. Blackbourne," Maggie reassured, but he continued on.

"You must believe me," he said quietly, though his eyes were as wide as if he were screaming. "Something is living in my house that I cannot see, and I think you are right. I believe this spirit murdered my Anne."

It was a moment before the full weight of his words settled upon her. "I do believe you," Maggie said at last.

Her eyes were drawn away from his as an elderly couple passed by. She realised only then how close they had gotten to one another. He too seemed to notice that he had been leaning over the table, and they each adjusted themselves more casually. "This is not the place to speak of such things," he said evenly.

"Will you meet me at this address in two days? We can discuss everything." Maggie quickly scrawled the address on a napkin and handed it to him.

He nodded, pocketing the napkin and standing as if they had only discussed something as mundane as the morning's weather.

"Shall I return you to your brother?" Charles suggested. "I wouldn't want for him to worry after you."

"Of course," Maggie said.

She took his arm, and he led her back into the dining room.

The table turned to her in surprise as she returned with her unexpected companion. Maggie felt some measure of childish satisfaction seeing the look on Richard's face as he saw she had not returned alone. In fact, in objective comparison to Charles, Camila's cousin wasn't as dashing as she had first concluded. His features were rather boyish for her taste.

"Maggie, It's good to see you're alright. Jonathan was becoming so worried," Camila said. "We were about to send a search party."

"No need," Maggie said fluidly. "I merely stumbled into an old friend, and we got caught catching up."

"I'm Jonathan Ward, Margaret's brother." He stood and extended his hand with narrowed eyes. "If we've met, I can't recall."

"Charles Blackbourne, I don't believe I've had the pleasure," Charles replied, shaking his hand. "But I'm afraid I've intruded enough for one evening." He nodded to her before turning away. "Ms. Ward."

Camila eyed her scandalously as she returned to her seat as casually as possible.

"Maggie, who was that?" Jonathan asked, glaring after him.

"Jonathan, weren't you telling me about your family's country estate?" Camila intervened.

Jonathan looked conflicted for a moment before he surrendered himself back into a detailed description of their childhood home. Maggie took a grateful sip of her champagne, still reeling from the unexpected turns of the evening.

CHAPTER

6

THE WEATHER WAS AS PICTURESQUE as one could wish of fall in New York. An unseasonably warm sun perched in the cloudless sky, easing the late autumn chill. This unexpected pleasure had redirected Maggie in order to walk through Central Park on her way to West 73rd Street. She had written to Walter for him to expect Mr. Blackbourne and herself at his offices there around 11 o'clock.

After two tedious, wholly uneventful days about the apartment waiting for the appointment, the quiet walk did her good. She had been unable to forget the haunted look in Charles's eyes, his mentions of strange occurrences. To think that a spirit was responsible for Anne's murder, was it even possible? However, such thoughts were hard to linger on as the sunlight brought to life the warm autumn colors around her. The park was crowded with couples walking arm in arm. Families played on the grass lawns. As

Maggie crossed the Bow Bridge, a few boats paddled over the waters littered with vibrant fallen leaves, peaceful and carefree. She stopped for a moment there, her pale skin drinking in the warm sunlight. Death and dread were strangers in a place like this.

Yet as Maggie emerged from the park back to the city's busy streets, her anxieties awaited her. Soon enough she would have answers, Maggie reassured herself as she crossed the street and began down the sidewalk of West 73rd. She immediately saw the offices of the American Society for Psychical Research. Sandwiched between two identical buildings, number 5 looked out onto the street through iron gated windows.

Though Maggie had not seen Walter in the weeks since their sitting with Charles, he had mentioned her in the journal as promised and thoughtfully sent her a copy. They had corresponded many times through letters in which he had invited her to come to the ASPR offices, an offer she had yet to accept, until today.

Maggie walked up the stone steps and through the door without pause. Inside, the walls were covered from floor to ceiling with shelves of books and pamphlets. To the left was a man sitting at a filing desk nearly hidden behind an enormous stack of papers. He was looking down at something in his lap, quite unaware of Maggie's entrance. She waited patiently for him to make note of her presence as she glanced over the scattered papers. However, they appeared to be disappointingly mundane. Maggie's curiosity led her to lean to see what was so interesting for the man at the desk to be studying. To her surprise and slight disgust, it was a magazine filled with drawings of women in various states of undress, all in ridiculously unladylike positions.

Maggie cleared her throat loudly, and the young man's neck snapped up to see her as he discarded the magazine quickly from view.

"Can I- Can I help you, miss?" he said, his voice cracking in panic.

"I'm here to see Mr. Davies," Maggie said pointedly, sounding eerily of many teachers she had known.

"Yes," he said quickly. "His office is upstairs." The young man pointed to the staircase on the far side of the room. Maggie nodded once in thanks, still casting a disapproving look.

Up the stairs was a long white hallway with a number of closed doors on either side. It was not difficult to find the one labeled Davies. Maggie knocked quietly.

"Come in," his voice sounded on the other side.

Maggie turned the old, stubborn knob and entered the small office. The room was packed to its capacity with oddities. Bizarre instruments and other various pieces of equipment were arranged haphazardly behind the door. A bookshelf to the left wall was stacked high with files and journals. To the right was a chalkboard filled corner to corner with some form of mathematics. His desk was covered in all sorts of graphs, lists of numerals, and many labeled audio recordings.

"Ms. Barlow." Walter stood to greet her, straightening his brown corduroy jacket.

"I'm so glad you got my message in time," Maggie said.

"Yes, you stressed that the situation was urgent?"

"I'm afraid I don't know much more than you at the moment," Maggie began. "Only that it involves Mr. Charles Blackbourne. Do you recall?"

"Yes, of course," he said eagerly. "You say his wife claims to have been murdered."

"Yes," Maggie nodded. "Well, our paths crossed two days ago, and he described, vaguely, happenings within his home, which he believes are of a spiritual and malignant nature."

"You believe him?" Walter asked, cleaning his glasses.

"For a skeptic to admit such a thing is not a simple feat."

"So you believe he may be the subject of a true haunting?"

"One would hope not, of course," Maggie said.

"Naturally." Walter straightened his glasses on his nose. "Well, I will show you to the research library. It will be more comfortable for us all there. I can assure you we can conduct our business there for the hour undisturbed."

"Of course."

Walter struggled to skirt around his cluttered desk and past her at a respectable distance in the small office. Finally, he succeeded in leading the way through the open door. Maggie followed him back the way he came into the lobby.

"You must have met our secretary, Mr. Barnes," Walter introduced.

Mr. Barnes nodded to them stiffly as they passed.

"Indeed," Maggie said, narrowing her eyes as Walter led her on toward a door at the back of the room. It opened into a quaint little library with a round table in the center. The windowless room was lit by a single electric light over the table.

Walter spent several moments fiddling with the record player as Maggie watched passively. It was not long at all before the young Mr. Barnes opened the library door. "Mr. Blackbourne for you."

Charles stepped through to meet them, taking his hat in hand. He was dressed in the same black overcoat which he had worn when they first met in her parlor.

"So good of you to come." Maggie greeted, feeling a wave of nervous energy which she tried at once to silence. "I'm sure you remember Mr. Walter Davies?" She motioned to where he stood over the record player.

Charles nodded in acknowledgement. "Yes, thank you for seeing me."

"It's nothing at all," Walter said. "Please sit."

As they each took a seat around the table, Charles's expression darkened as the familiar shadow fell over his eyes until they appeared somber, even tortured within.

"Would you mind if I record our conversation?" Walter asked.

Charles simply nodded.

Walter set the needle and began, "Hello, the date is November 22nd, 1916. I, Walter Davies of the ASPR, am here with medium

Maggie Barlow and her client to discuss possible paranormal occurrences within his home."

For a moment, only the scratchings of the record filled the silence.

"So, where would you like to begin?" Maggie asked. "Can you recall the first occurrence which made you feel as if something was not right?"

Charles sat back in the chair, looking down at his folded hands in contemplation. "I should say," he began, looking up at her. "It started with feelings that I believed to be only my own grief haunting me. Though, now that I look back, I knew then it was something more because that is what led me to you, the feeling that somehow, something of her was left behind. Her presence was not gone from our home, and I could feel in the deepest part of myself that she was still with me. Then, of course, you know what happened next. I came to you and simply could not believe what you had told me. My disbelief in you fueled my ability to call it all imagination. When I returned home, I packed everything that was hers away.

"It must have been only days later that I was woken in the night. It was cold, and I went to put another log into the fire when I heard the dog whining downstairs. It was unusual for her to make such a noise, so I went down to her. She stood by the kitchen door which led out into the garden. I opened the door for her, but she would not go through. Instead, she sat in the doorway nervously. I was sure then that something was in the backyard, perhaps a burglar or an animal of some kind. There was no one there but myself, but lying on the cobblestones was a dress, my wife's. I recognised it as the one which... which she had worn the day she fell.

"You must understand that I did not believe at that time that something abnormal was happening in my home. My maid, Ruthie, moved with me to the city from my parent's home in Virginia. I was quite sure this was nothing more than her coping with my wife's death in her own way, that she had set the dress aside when I asked her to pack up Anne's things. I was patient with this until I began to find the dress hidden throughout the house. One night I even found it laid out on my bed beside me when I woke. I knew then that I would have to speak with her. It wasn't until the next day that I had the chance, but she asked me then at breakfast why I had left it in her room and if I wanted her to pack it away in the attic again.

"I told her that morning to put it in a trunk with a lock, and she did." Charles paused for a breath, his story clearly taxing his nerves.

"Would you like some water, Mr. Blackbourne?" Maggie asked.

"Charles, please, and no. I should like to continue. Just give me a moment." Maggie nodded as Charles took a deep breath and soldiered on. "It was that night that I first knew something was very wrong. I woke to Ruthie's screams, and of course, I raced across the house to her, armed. The window in her room was shattered. Glass covered the floor and her bed. She had cuts on her arm and face from the shards. It took some time to calm her. She claimed the window had merely broken of its own accord, suddenly in a great cold breeze. I searched, but found not a rock or branch or other debris to suggest it had been broken. But that night, more troubling than her screams or the broken window, was the dress lying out in the garden. The next day I saw the trunk in the attic was still locked. The key was still in my possession, but the dress had somehow... I locked the dress back in myself that day.

"In the days following, the dress stayed in its place, but Ruthie was victim to many more unusual accidents. Around her, things would break, she would burn and cut herself while preparing meals. More than once, she fell down the stairs. I had her examined by a doctor. I feared that perhaps an illness had made her clumsy. Truthfully, I hoped it, but the physician could see nothing wrong with her. I had grown very concerned for her, for her safety. I told her that I would send her home, to Virginia, but she insisted she would not leave me. Perhaps I should have sent her anyway...

"It was after weeks of this that I decided that perhaps if there was no dress, there would be no more accidents. You must understand that after weeks of this terrorism, I was not in the fittest state. I burned the dress and sold the others and went to sleep that night in the hopes that the troubles were done... but they were not. I woke the next morning with an instant dread. I knew before my feet touched the floor that something terrible had happened. The garden, every flower of hundreds, had been cut. Each bud lay on the ground.

"I knew that no man could do this. It would take hours to prune an entire garden and such care not to trample a single one. You must forgive me for my behavior before. When I saw you, I had the foolish hope that I could blame you for this. But I know that you are right now. Something killed my Anne and now taunts me with the destruction of her memory… and I find myself wholly powerless to stop it."

It was as if the whole room took a breath of silence as Charles finished his story.

"Charles, I- We will discover a way to bring peace back to your home," Maggie promised.

"That is my greatest wish," Charles admitted.

"Thank you for coming in to see us. I'm sure the information you have shared will prove invaluable in solving not only your case but also in understanding events such as these better in the future," Walter said.

"Perhaps that will grant me some relief," Charles said with a polite smile.

"I believe it might be prudent for Ms. Barlow and I to come and see the house. I could bring some of my equipment, gather data if you will."

"Of course."

"We'll write you then?" Maggie suggested.

"Very well," Charles said as they all stood. "I thank you for your time, truly." He dipped his head and excused himself.

Maggie and Walter were quiet for a moment in his wake. Her hands twisted anxiously before her until she could not take it a moment longer.

"Please excuse me," Maggie said as Walter began to sit. He faltered as he was half seated but waved her off anyhow.

Maggie rushed through the lobby, unsure why she was running, why her heart was thundering with such urgency. Mr. Barnes looked up at her, startled as she pushed open the door. The sunlight was nearly blinding as Maggie took down the stairs, skirts in hand.

"Charles!" she called, seeing the shape of his black overcoat walking toward the park.

He halted his step and turned.

Maggie slowed her pace, though her heart was still hammering.

"Is something wrong?" he asked as they met.

"No, not at all," Maggie said. "I just, I came to make sure... I realised I'd never asked you if you were alright."

Charles looked over her at the others crossing on the sidewalk. He stepped to the side, and Maggie followed. His dark eyes studied her face for a time.

"Are you alright, Charles?"

He sighed. "No, I am not... but for the first time, I have hope that I shall be, someday."

Hollowness ached within her. "I will do everything I can." The words seemed so feeble, probably because she was unsure what she even *could* do.

"I believe you will," Charles nodded. The heavy sadness lingered in his features. Maggie wanted nothing more than to ease it, to see his eyes alight with laughter, or simply soft with contentment.

"I should return," Maggie said quietly.

Charles nodded. "I have my own appointments as well."

Despite his words, he lingered there on the sidewalk a moment longer until Maggie offered a small smile and turned back toward number 5.

Walter was seated in the little library, reading through his notes as Maggie entered.

"Truly amazing," Walter said without looking up, "his account is very detailed."

"Yes," Maggie agreed, taking a seat beside him.

"I found it intriguing, the spirit's attachment to the dress," Walter said.

"Yes, moving the dress about the house. It seems an intimidating behavior, don't you think?"

"Well, yes, of course, but more interesting still is the clear escalation in behaviors surrounding it. The dress is locked away and immediately, the spirit commits the first act of violence. It supposedly continued the aggression until the dress was burned and then the culling of the garden. It is a shame that the dress was destroyed. I would have liked to study it."

"Well, you can hardly fault him," Maggie said.

"Certainly not!" Walter nodded in agreement. "But I believe that it would be in the best interest of all to arrange an investigation of the house as soon as possible."

"You are sure I will be of use there?" Maggie asked.

Walter raised a brow. "Your presence there is indispensable, don't you think?"

"If you say so," Maggie said, shuffling. "It's only I wouldn't know what to do with myself. I've never encountered a haunting. I honestly didn't know if it was even possible. I've never even held a sitting outside my own parlor."

"If the spirit is trying to make contact so aggressively, perhaps your sensitive presence will draw it out. We should not ignore a chance to communicate."

"Of course," Maggie said. "You're right. I only worry with Mr. Blackbourne's hopes riding on us so heavily."

"We can only do our best to help, and perhaps in stepping away from your norms, you will surprise yourself."

Maggie weighed this in her mind, how far she had progressed even since she had begun her practice only some months ago. She found it much easier to approach the whispering veil, to focus on a single voice and draw it closer. A wonder came over her as she considered how much further she could grow. "Perhaps I shall."

CHAPTER

7

AS WALTER MARCHED PURPOSEFULLY off Park Avenue and down Warren Street, his eyes followed the house numbers diligently. The whole street was presided over by fashionable, though remarkably similar, townhomes. When at last he came to the correct address, Walter hopped up the stairs eagerly and came through into the hall. He turned at once to the door labeled 320 and knocked, very much hoping Maggie was in.

Maggie was indeed at home. In fact, as Mr. Davies ushered himself in from the cold, she was sitting on the settee, resigning herself to a wholly boring afternoon. Jonathan was with her, reading the paper and making occasional comments, to which she had no context and therefore were not really any basis for conversation at all. Maggie was just about to suggest that Jonathan invite Camila for dinner, so that she might have some small excitement to look forward to, when she was interrupted by two events. Firstly was her brother exclaiming, "Well, I would hope-" but whatever he was hoping for or against was additionally interrupted by Walter's unanticipated knock on the door.

Maggie was on her feet before she could think and opened the door before her brother had even managed to fold his paper.

"Mr. Davies," Maggie greeted. It had only been a day since their meeting at his offices. She had not expected to hear from him so soon, certainly not in person. He wore a slate grey suit with a blue knitted scarf wrapped around his neck. Even so, his cheeks were still ruddy from the cold.

"I am terribly sorry to come to you unannounced," Walter said, awkwardly stepping inside. "But I gather it is rather urgent."

"Urgent?" Jonathan repeated, standing from his armchair.

"What's wrong?" Maggie asked, ignoring him.

"Mr. Blackbourne requests that we come to the house immediately. Something happened there in the night. I don't know what, but he sent me a correspondence requesting our presence as soon as possible," Walter said quickly.

"Wait," Jonathan interrupted. "Mr. Blackbourne, from dinner the other night?"

"The very same," Maggie answered shortly.

"He is a... client of yours?" Jonathan said, clearly wincing at the idea of validating her occupation with such professional jargon.

"Stay out of it, Jonathan," Maggie snapped, hurriedly shoving her arms into her fur trimmed coat.

Walter stood by the door looking from one to the other in minor distress

"You can't just go out to a man's house alone!" Jonathan said, advancing on her.

"I'm not going alone. Walter will be with me."

Walter's face turned white as Jonathan's reddened.

"I will be back for dinner. You should invite Camila," Maggie said, ignoring Jonathan's protesting glare as she exited the apartment. "So where are we going?" Maggie prompted as Walter simply stared at the closed door through which they could hear Jonathan's muffled protests.

"Oh, yes, of course. Mr. Blackbourne provided me with an address uptown."

"We should call a car," Maggie said, walking out of the building and onto the street.

It was a short wait in the cold, but soon they were on their way to Charles's townhouse in the warmth of the cab.

"I do hope that I haven't caused any issue between you and your brother?" Walter asked.

"The only issue here lies with him," Maggie said. "I am quite my own person. Besides, someone has to bring this family into the twentieth century, for goodness sake."

"Quite right," Walter said, cleaning his glasses.

Soon they stood before a three story townhouse wedged between two other brick structures. It was topped with a charcoal slate roof. Each window was framed with the same dark color. Up

the stone steps was a polished cherry wood door which was secure behind an iron wrought gate.

Maggie braced herself against a cold wind as Walter rang the doorbell. Thankfully it was only a moment before the door opened, and Walter pulled open the gate to let her inside. A small Tiffany glass fixture cast a pale light down on them from above. She could not help but note Charles's appearance was more casual than she had seen him. His dark hair was untamed, revealing a natural wave and curl near the nape of his neck. He was without a jacket. The sleeves of his shirt had been rolled up his forearms. Maggie found it rather impossible for her eyes not to linger on the clearly defined cords of muscle that moved beneath his skin as he took her coat. Beneath, she wore a plain white blouse and a deep brown skirt. Maggie had not bothered with pearls or even a hat that morning, not expecting to leave the house. Likely for the best, she considered. This was hardly a social visit.

From a side room, a slender hound trotted gracefully into the hall, wagging its short, stumpy tail. Its coat was red, save for the feathery white hair that covered its belly. It looked between them cheerily.

"No, Lily," Charles said, pushing her back from Maggie's skirt. "Go lay down."

The dog followed his commands obediently and disappeared back through where it had come.

"I cannot say how grateful I am that you were able to come at such a notice," Charles said as Walter hung his hat.

"It was no trouble at all," Maggie replied. "But, tell me, what has happened? Walter told me the matter was urgent."

Charles glanced away, down the hall. There was a nervous energy about him, despite his polite manner, dread which spilled into her as well. "Well, yes. Unfortunately, I must say it is," he said darkly. "Please, this way."

Charles led them to the back of the house and through the kitchen with a purposeful stride but stopped as he reached a closed door. Apprehension filled his features as he lingered in the threshold.

"If you like, we can take a look for ourselves," Maggie offered.

Charles nodded his head concisely and stepped aside.

Walter opened the door slowly, and Maggie followed him within. She was quite unable to stifle herself as she let out a betraying gasp.

The maid's room was small, with a window that overlooked the courtyard garden. What once must have been a modest though comfortable residence was now in utter disarray. The night table was splintered on its side, discarded in the corner closest to the door. Up high on the wall, level to Maggie's head, was a splattering of dirt and below it the remains of a potted plant. Maggie nearly stepped on a shard of the shattered porcelain. The quilt on the bed had been ripped beyond repair as if savaged by a wild animal. All this was a mere footnote in her perceptions as Maggie's pale green eyes fixed widely on the wall over the bed. Scratched into the floral wallpaper was a single word: *MURDER*.

Walter circled the room wordlessly, taking in and absorbing each detail of the horrors which had no doubt taken place. Maggie simply stood in the corner, transfixed. Her hand still covered her mouth, but she could not seem to move it away.

"Ms. Barlow, are you alright?" Walter asked softly.

"I don't believe that anyone could be alright in this instance," Maggie answered, voice hollow and distant as she continued to process the morbid details.

"Quite right," Walter said, following her gaze to the terrible word. It was a moment before he spoke again. "Do you feel anything?"

Though she knew well the true meaning of his words, the only sensation that came to her was the chill of fear against her skin. She felt well and truly afraid. The thought of seeking out this... monster, making a connection between their minds. She couldn't bear it. Instead of saying as much, she simply shook her head.

Walter nodded. "I shall take some measurements here," he said decisively. "Then I should like to take some samples from the garden."

"Yes, of course," Maggie said. "I must apologise for being so useless."

"A tool for every job, my father always said." Walter offered her a small smile. "You'll find your purpose here yet."

Maggie smiled as well, though inside, she felt only a sickening twist in her stomach. With a deep breath, she collected her nerves and left Walter behind as he fiddled with his instruments. Charles had remained outside the door, his arms folded around himself tensely. He straightened as she emerged.

"Ms. Ward, I wished to speak with you, if you wouldn't mind."

"Yes, of course," Maggie replied.

Charles nodded and waved her toward the sitting room. It was a comfortable, intimate space. Impressionist paintings of forest scenes decorated the dark green walls. A pair of twin red armchairs were set before the fireplace. Over the mantle hung crossed antique rifles and a cavalry saber. Maggie noted a piano against the wall as she passed.

"It was Anne's," Charles explained as he offered her a seat.

"You said that she enjoyed music," Maggie recalled.

"Yes, she was quite gifted."

"I must say I admire that," Maggie said. "Despite years of tutors, I failed to develop an ear for it."

"The poor thing is probably out of tune now," Charles said mournfully.

"I- I'm sorry. I shouldn't have-"

"No, please," Charles exhaled and combed his hands through his loose fallen curls. "It is only I who must apologise. I've drawn you into something beyond what I have any right to ask of anyone, let alone..." He took a heavy breath. "No matter. I have decided that I will be leaving this house. I could use a leave of absence from my work as it is. I shall stay with my family in Virginia."

"Charles, I want to help you. Walter and I, we've come to-"

"You must understand," he said with such force that she recoiled slightly. "This evil has killed my- my wife. It's now threatened the life of my maid. I cannot put another in harm's way."

"Is she alright, your maid?"

He nodded in an unconvincing manner.

Maggie looked at him. The torment in his eyes was evident... and heart wrenching. Though her fear stirred riotously within her, she knew what she must do.

"I should like to keep my word to you," Maggie said firmly. "I said that I would try to make this home safe for you again. I intend to do so, a final effort."

Charles leaned back in his chair, pressing his fingers to his lips. "What do you suggest?"

"A sitting, here, tonight," Maggie said. When he did not answer at first, she added. "You would not have to attend if it would make you feel at all-"

"Of course, I would attend," Charles said dismissively. "But, Ruthie should be safely away. There has been far too much aggression toward her. I simply could not ask her to endure it again."

"That may be wise," Maggie allowed. "Has she spoken of last night's events at all?"

"She has done nothing since this morning but pray." His eyes cast up at her with a grim expression.

"And you?" What had seemed a simple, innocent question revealed itself far more intimate than she had intended as Walter entered the sitting room, the knees of his trousers stained with dirt.

"I've collected some samples and measurements, but nothing of real note yet," he said.

"Very good," Charles said, standing. Maggie followed suit.

"I was just suggesting to Mr. Blackbourne that we hold a sitting here, this evening."

"Yes," Walter nodded. "I think that is a rather good idea. Best not to wait."

"Would you-" Maggie began, turning to Charles. "Should I look in on your maid for you?"

"Her testimony as a first hand witness could be very informative," Walter said.

"I shouldn't have her interrogated," Charles said, hands returning to his hips.

"Certainly not," Maggie agreed softly.

He hesitated for only a moment before nodding. "She's lying down now in the guest room upstairs. I'll show you up."

Maggie nodded.

Upstairs was a single straight hall. All of the doors were shut but one. Through it, Maggie could see the maid, Ruthie, sitting on the bed. She was young, probably no older than Maggie herself. Though she was colored, she carried a rather fair complexion even so. Her hair was wrapped in a covering. She was still dressed in her nightgown, a blanket wrapped around her shoulders tightly. The maid had been muttering to herself but stopped and looked at her with round brown eyes as Maggie stood in the doorway.

She entered slowly. Ruthie's gaze flickered from her to Charles who remained in the hall until Maggie took a seat beside her.

"Ruth, is it? How are you feeling?" Maggie asked.

"There's a chill in the air, miss. It isn't natural."

"I'm here to talk to you about what happened," she prompted.

Ruthie's eyes fell to the floor, and she became rigid, unwilling to speak.

"I'm here to help. I can find out what it wants, and we can make it go away."

"It means to kill me," she said in a hollow whisper.

Maggie was lost for a moment at the bluntness of her statement, the numbness in her eyes. "Perhaps it would be better for you to find somewhere else to stay," Maggie suggested. "Until it is safe again for you here."

Ruthie's eyes grew wide and shot to where Charles stood in the hall. "You don't mean to send me away. I will stay. You don't mean it, sir!" Her breathing was rushed and frantic.

"Surely you don't want to put yourself in harm's way?" Maggie said.

Ruthie shook her head vehemently. "Mr. Charles needs me. It is my place. He needs me here."

Maggie nodded, seeing that pushing her any further would only lead her into hysterics. "You should rest."

Ruthie pulled the blanket tighter around her shoulders. "He wouldn't," she whispered so softly Maggie barely heard as she turned for the door.

Charles had led her back downstairs before she spoke again.

"You will make arrangements for her?" Maggie asked.

Charles sighed. "I have been trying to persuade her to return home to her family, but she refuses. She's very loyal to me."

"She certainly seemed so."

"Ruthie's been with my family since childhood, you see. She grew up with my brother, Malcolm, and I...she is like family to me. You understand?"

"I do," Maggie nodded.

"But you are right," he sighed. "I must find some accommodations for her. This house is no longer safe. She must go before tonight."

CHAPTER

8

MAGGIE RETURNED HOME to Jonathan's cold company, where she spent the rest of the afternoon. As soon as she stepped through the door, she could immediately sense the tense energy coming from her brother as he studied innocuous things with keen interest, determined not to acknowledge her. That is, not until it was nearly dark and Maggie announced that she would be back later.

Jonathan actually dropped whatever small object he had been holding. "You cannot be serious?" His eyes went wide as he stared her down, not even bothering to retrieve whatever had fallen.

"I am. I'll be back tonight. But this appointment is rather unavoidable."

"Camila will be here for dinner any minute!" Jonathan protested, fuming after her as she gathered the last of her things.

"Please make my apologies. Dine without me. I've already-" Just as Maggie was about to explain that she had snuck an ample portion of food from the kitchens in preparation, there was a knock at the door.

Jonathan looked between her and the door for several breaths, debating whether he could let her out of his sight for the thirty seconds it would take to stand on polite ceremony. Camila knocked again, and her brother let out a violent sigh as he marched to the door. Before Camila had even said hello, Maggie had slipped into her own coat and shoved her gloves into her pockets.

"Hello, I- oh!" As Camila stepped into the house, Maggie slithered behind her and out the door. "Maggie, where-?"

Her inquiry into Maggie's strange behavior was vehemently drowned by her brother's threatening utterance of her full christian name. "MARGARET JANE WARD!"

However, Maggie spared not a second to listen. The latter half of his proclamation was muffled by the closed door. She hailed a cab as soon as possible as she worked on her gloves. The night was positively freezing.

Once she was inside the cab, a flicker of guilt came over her. She would of course apologise to Jonathan when she returned. She knew full well what this must look like to him, another rash, irresponsible stretch of propriety, but there had been no use in explaining why she had to go.

All such notions were pushed from her mind as Maggie stepped out onto the nearly deserted street. The lampposts were lit now and shed pools of amber light on the sidewalk. Looking up to the house, its facade seemed more imposing. Perhaps it was the hour or her purpose in it, but nonetheless, a sense of foreboding crept over her. Yet after spending the entire afternoon gathering her courage, Maggie was far too proud to concede now. She took up the steps and rang the bell. Inside, the dog became excited by the commotion. Soon Charles was opening the door for her. Though he had amended his earlier disorderly appearance and now stood fully dressed and hair combed, a worrisome expression still creased his brow.

He took her coat quietly, greeting her only with a small smile.

"Thank you," she murmured out of pure reflex.

The dark green walls of the sitting room were nearly black in the dim light of the fireplace. Maggie could not help but catch the eye of a stuffed quail which looked back at her apprehensively. In the flickering of the firelight, it seemed almost as if it would take off at any moment.

Walter was standing beside an armchair. He turned to her wordlessly as Maggie stopped at the threshold. The room was quiet for several moments as the crackling of the fire provided an entrancing overture. A strange voice popped into the back of her mind, her mother scolding her; ladies do not hover in doorways. The thought was so surreally ridiculous that Maggie almost let out a scoff. For one thing, for all the issues her mother would draw from this evening, hovering would likely be at the bottom of an extensive account. And for another, of all the things to be afraid of tonight, her mother's disapproval held a similar position.

As they stood there, Maggie could feel the fear in the air, but also a readiness, a purpose. Each of them knew as soon as they spoke, a chain of events would begin which would force them to put aside their misgivings and push bravely into the unknown.

"Will you require any preparations?" Charles asked at last.

"It would be best," Maggie said more loudly than truly necessary, trying to shake herself to reason. "If we sit at a table small enough for us to join hands, preferably, in a room with a fireplace such as this for light."

"The table in the kitchen should do. You and I could clear some space in here for it." Charles said to Walter who promptly nodded.

The men pushed aside the armchairs and brought in the small breakfast table. It was covered with a cloth, and chairs were found for each of them. Walter then took some time setting up an array of his instruments. Charles began to pace the length of the room in silence, leaving Maggie to sit in one of the displaced armchairs, studying the delicate pattern of the lace tablecloth.

Walter cleared his throat to indicate he was finished, such a casual noise that almost made Maggie flinch. They each looked at one another once more, agreeing wordlessly to continue, before Walter put the needle on the record.

"Hello, the date is November 26th, 1916, and I, Walter Davies of the ASPR, am here with medium Maggie Barlow and her client who has sought Ms. Barlow's assistance in investigating paranormal happenings within his home since the death of his wife."

They sat alone, listening to the crackling of the fire, the scratching of the record. The only other sound was the blood pounding in her ears. Maggie took in a breath, not wanting to shake, as she joined hands with Walter and Charles.

They watched her, Walter's blue eyes set with determination beside Charles's grim and guarded expression. Maggie reached out her senses, slowly, tentatively, the way one reaches for the knob of a door late at night when they are unsure what they will find on the other side. She found it at once, the mist, the hazy veil between. It had always held a sensation of coldness, like a wintry draft. But here, in this place, the vapors were like ice caressing her skin. Maggie let out a gasp as her hair stood on end.

"Ms. Barlow?" Walter prompted her.

"Is she alright?" Charles followed.

Though her eyes were closed, she could hear the concern coloring his voice, feel his hand gripping her own tighter.

"I'm fine. I-" Maggie shuddered and swallowed. "It's very cold here."

"Can you continue?" Walter asked.

Maggie nodded.

"I am addressing the spirit living in this house," Maggie said in a loud, clear voice. With her mind, she reached into the frigid darkness.

There was no response, and then, like a shadow in the corner of her eye, something passed her consciousness. It was an eerie feeling, one she had never known before. To know that a spirit was *near*.

As she focused her mind, the whisperings grew quieter until she could sense only the presence that eluded her.

"Are you here with us now?" Maggie called again, wishing to draw it out. "If you can hear, knock twice to let us know you are with us."

It stirred. She felt it stir, consider. Two thundering pounds sounded against the ceiling. The grip on her hands became tighter, but neither of the men called out. Maggie realised her breaths were heaving, but as her focus turned back to her own body, her awareness of the spirit's movements began to fade.

"We are here to speak with you," Maggie said, forcing her mind clear and plunging back into the unnatural dark. "We know you wish to speak with us. Now is the time."

There were two more heart stopping pounds. It was circling closer now, the presence.

"Why are you here in this place?" Maggie called loudly as if to be heard over the roaring current of fear which raged through her.

The answer caused her hair to stand on edge as she found herself listening to horrible scratching, the sound of something sharp carving into the table before them. Maggie did not open her eyes. She would not let go, not now.

Suddenly she heard the tablecloth tear down the middle. Charles let out a strange noise between rage and terror as the lifeless halves of the cloth brushed past her hands, falling to the ground. Somehow, without needing to see, she knew what the spirit had written into the wood of the table. It was the same word that was now echoing endlessly about the mist. *Murder.*

Maggie pushed with all her will to regain her courage to speak once more. "Why must you murder? Why Anne? Why now Ruthie? What have they done to you?"

Maggie screamed.

She couldn't help it. The spirit seized her, pulling her deeper into the darkness until she was drowning in cold and dark, sheer nothingness that was as tangible as any force on earth. Beyond her, the tether to her body was like a single thread. The sitting room might as well have been another world, another life.

As her mind began to panic, searching for escape, a wave of anger overpowered her. Anger as a woman's body fell from a ladder, her skirts billowing as she fell too slowly to the ground.

Rage as she looked down at Ruthie sleeping in her bed. Fury which lashed out around her as the maid screamed, tearing and shattering and scratching.

It was all too much, the cold, the hate, the darkness. Maggie tried to struggle, to kick and fight as one would if they were drowning beneath the surface of a frozen lake. But the spirit held her. It wanted her to witness it, to feel the anger as the scenes played over again through her mind.

At last, Maggie took hold of that tether, memories of life, her life, and pulled.

It was like erupting from icy waters, like emerging suddenly from darkness into bright light. The shock of it ran through her, stealing her breath away as her eyes shot open. Walter and Charles's eyes were huge, looking down at her where she lay on the floor. Beyond them, she could see the flickering shadows of the firelight against the molding of the ceiling.

A moment passed, watching, before she could collect any sound. When the noise came at last, it collided with her, and Maggie realised that she was sobbing uncontrollably.

"Maggie?" Charles shouted as he shook her by the shoulders. Panic filled his brown eyes as they studied her face.

"Maggie, can you hear us?" Walter was feeling her pulse.

She pushed past the panic and took in a deep breath. "I- I-" Her chest still heaved with shuddering sobs, but Maggie tried to sit all the same.

"Don't move too quickly," Walter said.

"Should we call for a doctor?" Charles asked as his hand came to her brow, looking at Walter. "She's as cold as ice."

Another attempt at words came as nothing but gasping syllables and sobs.

"Just breathe," Walter instructed.

Maggie tried. She held onto one steady breath, then another. At last, Maggie began to stand. Charles wordlessly offered his arm as she found her footing. Walter took the needle off the record.

"You're freezing," Charles said, working off his suit coat and putting it over her shoulders.

His warmth lingered within, but the chill she felt was seeded deep within her bones.

"God, you're shivering." He pulled her against his body and began to rub her arms vigorously.

Some fragment of her mind thought to take issue with his touch, but she pushed the notion away and sunk deeper into his warmth. She needed to be near the thrumming of his heart, to feel that he was real, that he was alive.

"We must call for a doctor," Charles said. "There's-"

His voice was stolen as a resounding TWANG filled the room. One of the piano wires had snapped, and then another. From across the room, Walter's eyes widened in fright. Maggie could barely breathe as they all stood frozen from the terror of it. Though she was not reaching, Maggie stiffened as she felt the chill surrounding her. Her mind began to cloud, but she pulled herself back to her body, pushing herself deeper into Charles's warmth.

Maggie jumped, her entire body tensing with shock as behind her, the curtains began to shred, each seam tearing with a horrible rip. Discordant notes played on the piano, an overture of insanity.

All at once, without a word, they were running. The fire flared inside the hearth as they fled, splaying violent shadows across the wall. Charles was nearly carrying her as they made it to the hall. The dog was already scratching against the door as Charles threw it open, and they rushed down the steps.

They stood together panting for a moment, Maggie still tucked beneath Charles's arm. Outside, the house looked no different than it had been before. No evidence of the horrors that they had endured within. Its facade stood innocuously amongst the other homes, yet Maggie had seen its dark soul, and now she could not look away.

"It's time for me to leave this house," Charles said quietly.

Maggie straightened at his words, eyes flickering back. A shudder ran through her, not of cold, but fear. "I should be getting home," Maggie said. Her voice was flat as she shrugged off Charles's coat. The wintry breeze barely felt a tickle against her skin.

"I will take you," Charles said.

"No," Maggie said harshly but softened herself. "It's not necessary."

"I cannot let you go alone in your condition," Charles said. "By all accounts, I should be taking you to a hospital. At least let me take you home."

"I'm fine, really. I just-" Maggie lied.

"Ms. Barlow, he is right. You're in no state," Walter said.

Maggie found herself chewing on her lip, a habit she had thought she had dropped in her childhood. Finally, she nodded.

Charles walked her to the street. From there, she was in a car. She could not recall him hailing it, nor stepping inside. Walter was no longer with them, but she could not say where he had gone. Maggie said nothing as they rode. A terrible fatigue had come over her, her eyes hazily following the motions outside the window.

At last, the car stopped. Maggie felt like she had been woken from a trance. Her mind focused on each movement as Charles helped her down from the car, her apartment now before them.

"I am sorry for what happened tonight," Charles said, coming to a stop before the steps. "I never should have asked you to put yourself at such risk."

"Charles, no, I- It was me," Maggie fumbled, not meeting his eyes.

"Nothing that happened tonight could be your fault."

Maggie bit her lip again.

"You're shivering. Let me walk you in," he said, reaching out with a guiding hand.

"No," she said sharply, swiping it away. "I- I'll go alone."

"Will you let me check on you tomorrow?"

"I just need to sleep, then I will be-"

"Don't say that you're alright," Charles said, taking her arm. "You're not."

She stared at his hand on her bare arm. Her skin was covered with goosebumps, but she could barely feel the winter in the air. Inside, her heart thundered at his touch. Something deep within her wanted to latch onto him, to bathe herself in his warmth. To never let him go.

"I have to go," Maggie whispered. She'd already pulled him too far into the darkness. No more.

He released her, and Maggie went up the steps, turning as she reached the door. "Please just promise me- You can't go back to that house."

"I won't," he said solemnly, "but-"

She turned to the door to hide her face as unbidden tears began to bud in her eyes. "Goodnight, Charles."

Maggie closed the door behind her, leaving Charles on the street, alone. She could feel his eyes on her still as she leaned against the door and cried into the empty hall. Her powerlessness and cowardice consumed her from the inside out, and Maggie did nothing to stop them.

It was some time before her fatigue overtook her, outweighing all else. She straightened herself slowly. Maggie looked at the door to the apartment numbly, unsure exactly what she would find on the other side, only that she would have to face it to get to her bed.

"Where have you been?" Jonathan demanded, shooting to his feet as soon as the door closed behind her. Camila turned in her seat on the settee.

"Oh my, Maggie," Camila stood. "Where is your coat? What's happened?"

"I forgot it, I suppose." She could only imagine how she appeared. Her dark hair had fallen loose of its pins, likely in a state of utter disarray.

"Maggie, this nonsense has gone too far!" he bristled, thin lips taut in anger. "It can't go on like this, or I'll have to tell Mother and Father."

Maggie looked at him expressionlessly.

"You'll leave me no choice," he added, clearly at a loss. He had threatened to do the worst, but at this moment, it didn't seem to matter at all.

"Maggie, what happened?" Camila asked softly.

"There's nothing to tell," Maggie said, ignoring her and pushing past her brother. "I'm done with it. All of it. I'm done."

CHAPTER

9

MAGGIE CARRIED OUT THE tray of bite size cakes into the crowded dining room with a proud smile. As she set them in the center of the table, there was a murmur of excitement as many eager hands reached out to snatch one of the tasty morsels.

"Maggie, this is all too lovely," Camila said, looking around the apartment's sitting room which was now buried beneath Maggie's many accommodations for the party.

Ribbons had been hung from the ceiling and in the doorways. Trays of foods, savory and sweet, covered every surface. A mountain of gifts brought by the many admiring guests lay stacked neatly on the corner table, and filling every available crevice were bouquets of lilac and other dusty purple flowers which left a sweet aroma in the air. The small room had been filled to its absolute brim with extravagance, nearly to the point of making it seem cluttered. Many of the guests had taken to sitting or standing in the dining room instead.

"I tried to restrain him, Camila, but Jonathan insisted on throwing the party of the year," Maggie said playfully.

As the dreadful December weather carried on, it had become clear that there would be no leaving the city that year, especially not to Camila's family home in the country. So, Jonathan had nobly taken up the mantle of throwing Camila's birthday party. Maggie had volunteered for the cause gladly, seeing as her brother was hopeless when it came to parties. Not to mention she had desperately needed something to occupy her attention.

"What?" Jonathan said, seeming affronted. "I shall have you know that this circus was not my doing."

"It wasn't?" Camila asked.

"Well, it was my idea for the flowers," he admitted proudly.

Camila placed an endearing hand on his arm. The two of them had certainly become close over the past two months together. Maggie was pleased for them. At least somewhere inside herself, she was. Camila was a great friend and more than she had ever hoped for in a prospective sister-in-law. Doubtlessly, she would make Jonathan happy if matters came to that. Yet as Maggie's mind began to drift from the conversation about differing species of flora, she felt nothing especially at all, only the aching hollowness which found her whenever she was alone or her mind became unfocused.

And seated there, in her own sitting room, surrounded by at least twenty people, including her brother for Heaven's sake, she felt the touch of the void. A frigid whispering on her skin, cold and calling. Maggie's body seized, going rigid in protest. She pushed the sensation away as her heart raced against the creeping chill. Maggie tucked a loose curl behind her ear self consciously, hoping no one had sensed the sudden fear which had swept over her.

This sensation had come over her often over the past weeks, the feeling as if she were standing in the very shadow of death. Ever since that night at Mr. Blackbourne's home, when she had truly learned the danger of these forces with which she had meddled. It was as if the void wanted her back, but she would not follow. She was strong enough for that, at least, to turn her back on the whispers of the darkness.

When the feeling had all but passed, Maggie straightened and reoriented herself with her surroundings, taking stock of where the conversation had drifted without her. They were still crooning over the party.

"Don't forget that outrageous gift you bought for her," Maggie said coyly.

Jonathan's face reddened as Camila smiled widely.

"Outrageous?" Camila repeated to him.

"Well, I would hardly call it that," he said defensively.

The gathering began chittering and wondering amongst themselves.

"Oh, I can't wait any longer," Camila said jovially. "Maggie, you mustn't tease me this way."

"I think," Maggie said to the expectant crowd, pausing for effect. "Now is the time for Camila to receive her gifts." There was a brief applause. "But, I am under strict order from your mother that you must open their gift first."

Camila laughed as Maggie brought over the gift in a long garment box. She knew already what was inside, having picked it up from the post office and repackaged it with a pink ribbon a few days before. There was a flurry of whispers as Camila untied the bow, followed by silence as she lifted the lid and unfolded the paper, giving out a gasp of surprise. She lifted out the coat to a glorious chorus of admiration from the party.

"Put it on!" The crowd called, and Camila obeyed.

She looked as though she had stepped right out of a magazine from Paris. The tailored wool fitted around her perfectly and was finished with a fur collar and cuffs. Inside the box was also a fur hat to complete the ensemble.

The ladies surrounded her, examining the coat and complimenting it, asking her how it fit and feeling the soft fur. Maggie took her leave to stand at the edges of the room, still reeling and quite thankful to be out of the public eye. It had been an easy task to assemble a gathering of Camila's friends and admirers, mostly from her church and numerous social causes. Yet Maggie knew so few of them personally. She was hardly in the mood for polite conversation anyway. Instead, she took a cocktail from the table and began nursing it heavily. The warmth snaked through her veins, chasing away the chill and setting her more at ease.

Maggie paid little attention as the rest of the gifts were opened, though none were such a spectacle.

"Well, that can't be all," Camila said as she came to the last. "I haven't seen yours! You two stop teasing me! Where is it?"

"Oh, Jonathan, do put her out of her misery," Maggie said.

"Alright," he said in such a way that Maggie knew meant he was enjoying himself immensely. "I'll go fetch it then, shall I?"

Jonathan left for his room, leaving the many guests to whisper and Camila to wait, nearly jittering with excitement. He returned with a rare smile spread generously across his face as he presented the lavender gift box to her, and she opened it eagerly. The whole room appeared to be craning just to get the first peak at the contents inside.

"Oh, Jonathan, this is lovely," she said, taking out an intricately carved, antique cherry jewelry box.

"It was our grandmother's," Maggie said.

The old bat had never let her or her brother touch the thing or really anything of hers. It was odd even now, the old woman six years gone, seeing Camila inspect it. Maggie half expected to hear her grandmother scolding her about fingerprints from beyond the grave. She took another drink as she considered the horrible notion of actually hearing any such thing.

"It's so beautiful," Camila said.

"Open it," Jonathan said, clearly unable to contain himself a moment longer.

Camila gave him a fleeting look of happy surprise as she opened the lid, but it was consumed by awe as she looked on without words. The whole room was silent.

"Oh, Jonathan," she said finally, taking out the pearls gingerly and lifting them so the crowd could see.

"It's ten strands," Jonathan commented, looking positively tickled with himself.

"It's..." Camila began but seemed unable to find the right word to finish.

"Here," Jonathan offered, helping her to fasten the clasp.

They were truly exquisite, draping from her neck down and past her chest in even, lustrous strands.

"They're gorgeous," Pauline praised enviously.

"You look just like Queen Mary," Susan noted to everyone's agreement.

"Thank you," she said, her brown eyes practically sparkling as she gazed up at him.

Jonathan leaned down to kiss her sweetly on the cheek. "Happy Birthday, darling."

Maggie was just thinking of an excuse to step away when the bell rang. She slipped out as the guests continued to chatter about the necklace and what a fine match Jonathan and Camila would make. Maggie worked on her coat, unwilling to open the door to the cold without its protection. As she opened the door, her mind was far away and entirely unprepared to see Walter standing before her, hunched against the icy wind.

"Oh, I am so sorry not to write," he said, straightening his glasses, "but I was rather worried when you did not respond to my last letters."

"Walter," Maggie said, too surprised to utter anything else. He had written to her many times over the past weeks. She had read the first, asking if she was well, if she would be willing to meet to discuss the events at the Blackbourne house. The answer to both had been an emphatic negative. The rest of the letters she had ignored, like the coward she was.

"I must say that I was concerned for your well being," Walter explained further. "You were in a state that night. I've felt rather guilty for not seeing you home."

"Oh, I am fine, really," Maggie said as casually as possible.

"That is a relief. I was wondering if you would agree to a recorded interview of your experience? I was reviewing the data my devices gathered during the event and-"

"Walter, this really isn't the time. I'm entertaining."

"Oh, I'm very sorry. When would be a better time for us to speak?"

"I'm sorry. I'm afraid that won't be possible."

"Surely-" Walter began, but Maggie pressed on.

"I have other matters that require my attention at the moment."

"Don't you think it might help, to talk about what happened?" Walter asked, flustered.

"I am quite sure," Maggie said firmly. "Good day, Mr. Davies."

Maggie shut the door, shielding herself from his look of surprise and worse, concern. It was a terrible feeling knowing that he stood just beyond the oak barrier, a clawing reminder of everything she had spent weeks trying to ignore. The memory of how she had done the very same that night, shutting Charles away in the cold, barreled over her. The shame came up to her throat, choking her as tears threatened to overcome her.

She just needed a moment to collect herself. Moments came and went, and she found herself quite unable to move. Reentering the party was unthinkable as she teetered on the edge of a collapse she had been stalling for weeks.

"Maggie," Camila called, popping her head out of the apartment door into the hall. "It seems like everyone is getting ready to leave."

Maggie forced a smile onto her lips and nodded. Camila eyed her strangely as Maggie followed her back inside. But she said nothing as they each offered pleasant goodbyes and thank you's to all who had attended. After an hour or so, Maggie found herself lounging in the seemingly empty sitting room. Jonathan and Camila were locked in happy conversation about the party.

"Maggie," Camila said, catching her off guard. "Who was it at the door earlier?"

"No one, they had the wrong address," Maggie lied weakly.

They were all quiet before Camila spoke again. "Maggie, we've been wanting to talk to you. You've not been yourself lately, and when I saw you in the hall, you looked close to tears."

Jonathan straightened into the guise of the protective older brother, glancing sideways at Camila. Clearly, this was news to him.

Maggie simmered. She hated being under the microscope of their pity. "I am perfectly well," she said too forcefully to be believable.

"Does this have to do with Mr. Blackbourne?" Jonathan asked. "Was he bothering you?"

It was all Maggie could do not to growl in frustration. "No, Jonathan. I haven't spoken to Charles in weeks."

"Charles?" her brother bit out pointedly.

"What we mean to say is that you've been very mysterious lately. You haven't said a word about what happened that night, but we can both see that it's bothered you."

"I'm not being mysterious. There are just things I do not want to discuss," Maggie debated.

Jonathan scoffed loudly, but they ignored him.

"Jonathan says you haven't had an appointment since. I just don't understand. Your work was so important to you. You seem so unhappy these days, and we want to help."

"I know that this has something to do with Blackbourne. I'm sure of it, Maggie!" her brother insisted.

"Jonathan, please." Maggie stood, halting him before he could go any further. "Look at me when I say you are wrong. He is a client and nothing more. He's done nothing to upset me. I am done with the spiritualism business because I am bored with it. It tires me now. I shall have to find something else to occupy me in the future."

Maggie left them for her bedroom. It wasn't until the door was shut securely behind her that she felt as though she could finally breathe. She hadn't satisfied any of their concerns. That much was clear. This wouldn't be the end of their meddling either, but as Maggie curled herself into her bed, she could hardly find it within herself to care at all.

CHAPTER

10

THE MORNING SUN WAS JUST peeking over the buildings to shine down on the courtyard. Though an early morning chill lingered in the air, she relished the feeling of warmth against her cheek. Maggie reached for a fresh pink rose. The whole archway was in perfect bloom with the Eden roses. Their delicate petals were full and vibrant, filling the air with their floral scent. She reached deep into the eaves for the stem and clipped it with the shears. It joined the others in the basket hanging from her arm. Her brother would be here soon. She planned to set them out fresh in the guest room for him.

No.

That wasn't right. Jonathan was already here, asleep in his bedroom in their apartment.

Their apartment.

Maggie gazed down at the flowers in the basket. Below the ladder, the cobblestones were scattered with the garden clippings. This wasn't her garden, wasn't her home. It wasn't her.

In very the moment her memory returned to her, Maggie felt something ripping her down from the ladder. A scream built in her throat, but before it could escape, she was swallowed by darkness. Panic hammered at her chest as the cold seeped into her bones, as the emptiness engulfed her senses. The warmth of the sun, the smell of the roses, it was all gone.

Maggie thrashed against it. She screamed, but nothing swayed the silence, the stillness that was determined to remain. Her breaths came in desperate pants. Maggie forced herself to focus on the rising and falling of her chest. She was breathing. Her heart was beating. She was alive. Maggie clung to these thoughts, and they led her back to memories of warmth, of home.

All at once, Maggie was standing in the hall outside her own apartment. Beyond the glass of the door, the world was black, and she knew that the void lay just beyond. Slowly, the doorknob began to turn. She raced to hold it shut at once.

"Maggie," Walter's voice came from the other side. The knob struggled in her grip. "I just want to talk to you. Open the door."

She couldn't. If she opened the door, she'd be lost again.

A force pounded against the door, causing her to cry out as she drove the weight of her body against it. "You promised." Charles's voice sounded on the other side, punctuated by more thunderous bursts. "You promised me! Open the door."

Maggie shook her head, biting her lip as she held it shut with all her strength. She couldn't, not again.

It was utterly dark when Maggie jerked awake. Her skin was slick with a cold sweat, her breath coming quick and urgent. She fumbled for several moments with the matchbox trying to light her lamp before its warm glow filled her bedroom. Only then did Maggie realise that she was trembling.

This was not the first of her nightmares. Most of them concerned that night, but they had never felt so real. Never before had she had cause to fear if she had slipped unconsciously beyond the barrier. The thought was more troubling than she cared to admit.

Maggie swung her legs over the bed. It was too cold for her to sleep here anyway. She worked on her dressing gown and carried the lamp with her as she went out to the sitting room. Distant light from the street lamps poured in the windows, casting patterned shadows over the floor. It took some time to fix a proper fire, but as the flames built, they chased away the troubles echoing in her mind. Maggie sat before the mantle for several moments, feeling the heat against her skin.

Fatigue weighed heavily on her eyes as Maggie curled into a throw blanket on the settee. Altogether without meaning to, she fell into a dreamless sleep by the warmth and flickering light of the fire.

Mrs. Doyle found her there early in the morning, and though she gave her a disapproving eye, she made no move to wake her.

Sometime later, when his breakfast was already set on a tray in the kitchen, Jonathan emerged from his bedroom dressed for work.

He paused first in surprise but then taking in the sight. His sister was half upright in a heap of dressing gown and blankets. Her curly hair was in disarray, her arm jutting out awkwardly beneath her head. Jonathan had been working late the night before and was sure that she had gone to sleep before him, and in her own room. She must have moved in the night. Why he couldn't understand.

Ultimately, he decided to leave her to rest after what was likely a fitful night. As usual, Jonathan took his breakfast and coffee at the table, none of it disturbing Maggie's sound sleep. He gave Mrs. Doyle instructions not to wake her and left for work.

Jonathan prided himself on being a diligent worker. He liked his life in careful order. Family and work should remain separate, the border between them clear. It was no less than he would expect if he were an employer, but today, he found his mind wandering often. His concern for his sister had only grown since that night, which she categorically refused to speak of. What could have been so horrible that she wouldn't talk about it, even to him? He let out an aggravated sigh unnatural to his quiet office. Of that, he had several ideas. Yet, despite his worst imaginings, she was clearly suffering. Maggie was a ghost of herself, and she wasn't hiding it nearly as well as she seemed to think.

As Jonathan made his way home, he resolved to do something about it.

"For goodness sake, Maggie," Jonathan exclaimed before he was even fully through the door.

She had not moved an inch from where he had found her that morning, dressing gown and all. Maggie straightened herself on the couch and rolled her eyes, though she couldn't fault him too much. At this hour of the day, and out in the sitting room no less, she really was pushing the boundaries of acceptable dress. But this morning, she had simply been unable to find the will to fit herself into her usual rigid attire, or to do much of anything, for that matter.

"I'm decent," Maggie grumbled.

Jonathan hung up his hat and set down his case. "Really, I thought that infernal habit of yours was bad, but this- This is worse."

"I have a cold," Maggie rebutted.

"So she says," Mrs. Doyle commented, coming into the sitting room with the tray of tea that Jonathan always enjoyed after work. "I've heard not a sneeze."

Maggie eyed the traitor through dangerous slits.

"You've been sulking for too long," Jonathan said in a conclusive tone that filled her with dread.

"I'm just between engagements. I'll-"

"We're going out for dinner tonight, Mrs. Doyle," Jonathan said to the housekeeper.

"Of course, Mr. Jonathan," she said, leaving the sitting room standing a few inches taller than her short stature should allow.

Maggie sulked. "I'm really not feeling-"

"For the love of your brother, go and get dressed, Maggie," Jonathan said, pinching the bridge of his long nose.

She shut her mouth and eyed Jonathan for a moment. He so rarely dug his heels in this way. She found it difficult to argue with him, which she could never remember being an issue before.

Two hours later, they were stepping out of a cab onto the snowy sidewalk. It was strange, being fully dressed in her evening gown on the windswept street when only hours ago she had been curled in a most comfortable heap beside the fire. Her body went through the familiar motions as she relinquished her fur coat at the door and Jonathan pulled her seat out at the table.

Maggie had dressed in one of her favorite evening gowns. The rich green silk was accented with dark embroidery and beading. The back cut in a low reaching arch. She had hoped that the dress would have given her some excitement that evening, but all she could think of was the discomforting chill against her exposed skin and the way the bodice confined her figure.

When the waiter came, Jonathan ordered them both a decent vintage of champagne. As she took the first bubbling sip, she thought that perhaps this little venture wasn't wholly without reward.

"I'm going to ask Camila to marry me," Jonathan said importantly.

Maggie used every tool that finishing school had equipped her with not to spit her champagne across the table. Thus, she went into a coughing fit, barely able to force out the words "Jonathan- That's- That's- Wonderful."

"I am glad you think so," Jonathan said, the corner of his mouth playing with a smile. "I am rather pleased you both get on so well, though I think at times you are a wild influence on her."

"Dear brother, your would-be bride is more wild in her own right than you give her credit."

Jonathan pursed his lips and took a drink. "Nevertheless, I am very fond of her. I plan to propose at the Christmas party."

"So soon?" Maggie asked.

Jonathan simply nodded.

"So she is staying in the city for the holiday?" Maggie asked.

"She said the weather simply wasn't right this year," Jonathan explained.

"Oh, she's staying to be with you. It's obvious."

Jonathan reddened slightly. Maggie stifled a chuckle. She'd never seen him like this with a girl. He was ordinarily so businesslike with his courting. But Camila had always been special.

"Do you have a ring?" Maggie asked.

"Well, I supposed I would wait and let her choose one herself. I wouldn't know where to start-"

"Jonathan, no!" Maggie gasped in horror. "It's so unromantic to pick out your own ring. You have to dazzle her with your proposal. You need a ring!"

"Well if you feel so strongly-"

"I do! I'm going to take you out shopping, tomorrow. We'll pick one together."

"If you insist, alright," he said, nodding.

They spoke for some time about his plans, what he intended to say and where. It seemed he had given the proposal a good deal of thought, though Maggie added a few womanly suggestions.

"There was another matter that I wanted to broach with you tonight," Jonathan said as they began their entrees.

"Go on then," Maggie said tentatively.

"Well, it concerns my office," Jonathan said.

Maggie's back straightened, but she said nothing.

"As you said the other day, you do not plan to continue hosting your sittings in the upstairs office. If that is the case, I should hate to see the space wasted."

Maggie gritted her teeth. It had been weeks since she had hosted a sitting or even entered her parlor, but the idea of dismantling it, turning it back into the doldrum office of a banker; it twisted her stomach.

"At least consider it," her brother said when she failed to provide to the conversation.

"I suppose I was just thinking I might use it for something else in the future," Maggie said finally, popping a bite into her mouth.

"Oh? Such as?"

"Well, I don't know at present, but I..."

123

"I should like it back by the new year," Jonathan said conclusively. "That is unless you have other plans."

"Fine," Maggie said, stabbing a piece of fish rather forcefully.

Her agitation overtook her all the way through dinner and the cab ride home. Jonathan seemed to recognise that she was in no mood for companionship and kept quietly to himself. In fact, they didn't share another word for the rest of the evening besides a mumbled goodnight when Jonathan retired to bed, leaving Maggie alone in the dim sitting room.

Though she longed to undress and curl into her bed, she couldn't bring herself to sleep just yet. She turned abruptly toward the door and marched up the steps to her parlor. For what purpose, she was not sure. Maggie had no intention of ever hosting a sitting again. She couldn't possibly... not anymore. Yet, Maggie opened the door slowly, with care, and glanced inside.

She breathed in the scent of her incense. Her eyes traced over it all, the three stuffed crows and the wardrobe, the purple velvet curtains, and the old sewing table. The grandfather clock ticked idly in the corner. Though she could not bring herself to step inside, Maggie could not imagine packing it all away.

CHAPTER

11

JONATHAN HAD DRIVEN them out to one of the sprawling old money mansions on Long Island for what was likely to be a garishly extravagant holiday party. As they entered the ballroom side by side, Maggie's suspicions were proven entirely correct. Garlands hung from the columns about the dance floor. The band was just coming together to begin the waltz that would carry them all through the night. The wooden floor was polished enough to reflect the shoes of the many guests milling aimlessly about, chattering to one another in festive spirit.

Her warm velvet gown fit right in, red as the holly berry wreaths. It was a simple design that hung off her shoulders effortlessly, hugging her figure until it spilled to the floor in a brief train. Mrs. Doyle had fussed over her hair, feeling generous in the holiday spirit perhaps, and had littered it with small glittering adornments which looked like oversized snowflakes.

Even so, it was doubtful anyone would notice her tonight in Camila's company. Her dress was a light blush with layers of gauzy fabrics, which moved airily about her as she walked. The necklace Jonathan had gifted her hung from her neck, draping over the front of the dress in row after row of even, lustrous pearls. The blending of pink and ivory brought out the warmth of her skin tone and accentuated the rosy hue of her cheeks. Beside her, Jonathan wore his best suit, angular and clean cut without a wrinkle in sight. He leaned in and whispered something in her ear which reduced her to a fit of girlish giggles. They were a handsome couple to be sure and happy, truly sublimely happy.

Maggie sought out a cocktail and was readily supplied with one from a passing gilded tray. She took a long sip, watching as Jonathan led Camila to the dance floor with eyes only for her. It was an important night for them, Maggie reminded herself. She could not think why he had insisted she come, though being in the apartment on Warren Street alone on Christmas would arguably have been more dismal. She took another sip of her cocktail. At least that was good.

Couples paired up for each of the dances as Maggie nursed her drink alone. She was becoming a wallflower, rather unlike herself really. Then a horrid realization struck her. It was almost like she missed the forced company of her parents' arranged gentlemen. She had grown used to having a man to escort her, however dreadful he may be. At least she could make private jokes at their expense to occupy herself with. Without one, she found herself utterly lonely.

Her eyes swept the floor again. Surely if she straightened herself, became more lively, someone would notice her and ask for a dance. Admittedly, she was in a pathetic mood, but she scanned the room demurely nonetheless.

"Ms. Ward?" a gentleman's voice sounded behind her.

Maggie's attention had been so focused across the room that she whirled from the shock. Charles stood behind her, trussed up in his white tie. His black hair was slicked and showed no sign of its curl. Somehow his demeanor seemed wholly casual, but how could it be?

Her mouth opened, and she waited for some rehearsed pleasantry to escape her lips, but it seemed that even that was beyond her.

"Would you come with me?" He spoke so low his lips barely moved. His dark eyes watched the dancing pairs innocuously as he awaited her reply.

Maggie's mind was working at decidedly unhealthy speeds. At once, she regretted the cocktail. This was hard enough without the haze of intoxication. Or perhaps it was made easier as she found herself nodding in spite of the sound reason her sobered mind possessed.

As they exited the ballroom, his hand took her own, leading her down the hall. Her heart was about to burst. Her mind still struggled to process if this was indeed actually happening. Yet, she kept her expression as neutral as possible for the benefit of the merry passersby, even though they weren't paying them any mind anyway.

All at once, Charles took a sharp turn, leading Maggie into a small, darkened tea room. The sounds of the party were distant to the point of insignificance as they stood together in the dim light. They might as well have been on their own planet, and yet, to her great annoyance, she still could not think of a single word to say. Her language had failed her entirely. The frustration at the sheer betrayal of her faculties brought hot tears to her eyes. The fury that she had actually begun to cry egged them on until she was left with only a pitiable expression and a steeply growing self hatred.

All the while, he stood there staring at her, brow furrowed in an expression she could not hope to decipher in her present state.

She couldn't stand it for another moment. "I'm sorry," Maggie choked as she made a desperate break for the door.

Charles stepped to block her path as his hands found her shoulders. They held her firmly, but she could feel it in his touch that if she were to move away again, he would not stop her. And so they stood, her breaths coming too fast, his eyes never leaving her.

What did he want? It didn't matter whatever it was. She had to go. "Charles, I-"

His grip softened, lingering on her bare shoulders. "No, please. I wanted to speak with you... about that night. I should have-" Charles huffed. "I have thought of writing to you countless times, but I didn't want to intrude."

"I've been well enough. I've put it behind me and..." Her words sounded false to even her own ears. Her eyes fell to study the details of his lapel. "Have you found suitable lodging in the city?" Maggie asked quietly, punishing herself furiously within that she hadn't thought of something charming or clever in the slightest.

Charles released her and straightened. "Yes, I did find a small apartment that has suited me just fine."

Maggie nodded.

"Are you well, Maggie?" Charles asked, his dark eyes piercing her.

The air had vanished from her lungs as her heart hammered on. Perhaps an hour ago, she would have said yes, but now it was a decided no. No, she was not well at all. In fact, now that she really thought of it, she was rather unwell. And then she remembered herself, where she was, in a dark room, alone, with a gentleman. Her brother must be looking for her by now. If he found her like this, he would tell their parents, and then her goose would be more than cooked. It'd be scorched. "I have to go," Maggie said, though she did not move.

"Stay, please," Charles said so softly.

"I-"

Charles's eyes fixed on her lips, and she realised they were parted, waiting. He came to her, hand on her cheek as his lips met hers. Whatever shock should have swept over her never came. Part of her had been waiting for this, tensed and ready. Certainly not her rational mind, but she was sure that she had left that behind in the ballroom.

His touch was painfully tender, tentative, and wanting. It was going to kill her.

A whining sigh escaped her throat as she gripped his jacket tight in her fists. An answering growl rumbled through his chest as he pulled her in. Suddenly she was overwhelmed by his warmth, by his urgent touch as his fingers gripped her arms as if he was holding on for dear life. Maybe he was.

Charles's lips parted from her own as he let out a hot sigh. He took a step back, hands slipping from her arms. Maggie moved with him, not wanting their touch to end. But then he was standing a few paces away, hands on his hips, taking deep, even breaths. Maggie found herself rather speechless under entirely different circumstances.

"I must apologise for my behavior. That was terrible of me. I took advantage, and-"

"I wouldn't say that," Maggie said in a small voice.

His dark eyes flickered to her. They lingered trapped within one another's gaze.

"I shouldn't have pushed you away," Maggie whispered. "I- I promised to help you."

Charles was before her in a single stride. "It was horrible of me to even ask- What you experienced that night... It's my fault and no one else's. I never should have put you through that."

Maggie had never been one to cry in front of others, certainly not in a man's company. She despised women who opened and shut like faucets for their attention. Nonetheless, and quite beyond her control, Maggie began to sob in earnest, spilling tears into his jacket. Chest shuddering with struggling breaths. His arms held her tightly, never faltering.

At last, she took in an even breath. She sniffed, collecting herself before she lifted her eyes to his own. Charles was watching her silently. Without allowing herself time to think, Maggie raised herself onto her toes and caught his lips with her own. His eyes grew wide for a single moment before he melted around her.

This embrace was so unlike the last. Then her body had been as rigid as his grip on her arms. Now, they were molten, hot and fluid. Every sense was piqued as she felt his hands graze over the velvet of her dress, leaving trails of fire across her skin. She felt his tongue trace her lips, tasted the heat of his breath against her own. It was utterly unlike any touch she had ever known, and when they came apart, part of her wished to grab his collar and demand for more.

Instead, Maggie took in a breath of air. Her head swam with heated desire, his touch decidedly more intoxicating than any drink.

"Charles," Maggie whispered.

He let out a lengthy exhalation, resting his forehead against her for the briefest moment. "I should return you," he said, voice forcefully even.

The thought of returning to the party, to be seen by others and be again under the weight of what was proper, there couldn't be anything worse. Something had been released from her, feelings that she only now realised had been fighting to make their way to the light for some time. Emotions that she had no desire to expose to the merry gathering which lay beyond this darkened sitting room.

"Charles, I-" Maggie began, but he read her meaning plain.

"Sit down," he said, waving her into a chair. "Take the time you need."

Maggie sat, sinking into the chair without thought of propriety.

"If you want, I can leave you," Charles offered chivalrously.

Maggie shook her head. "No, please."

He nodded and took a seat in the armchair opposite.

"I've been horrible," Maggie said at last.

"Ms. Ward-"

"I do believe we are at the point of using one another's christian names," Maggie said pointedly.

Charles looked down, seemingly to hide a blush. "You haven't been horrible."

"Nonetheless, I can see now I have amends to make."

"Not to me," he said sincerely.

She offered him a small smile. They sat in companionable silence until Maggie stood suddenly. Enough really was enough, she could only indulge herself so far. Already she risked flying much too close to the sun. The thought of heat brought back the sensation of his body against her own.

"I- We- My brother-" Maggie stammered. Her fists clenched by her side.

"Would you like to dance?"

"I would," Maggie said evenly.

She checked her reflection in the mirror hanging from the wall, wiped her eyes, and fixed a few stray hairs. It wouldn't do to emerge looking like she had succumbed to her passions... twice. Maggie stifled a chuckle as Charles peered out the door to be sure the hall was empty. He waved her through, and she bustled from the room, biting her lips now to keep herself from a wildly betraying grin.

The ballroom was invasively loud, boisterously full, altogether the opposite of their private little sitting room. Charles took her hand, and she could see in his eye a conspiratorial agreement. She smirked and followed him onto the floor.

Maggie was an exceptional dancer, a perfect marriage of harsh mannered instructors and her own natural gift for movement. As the waltz began, her feet moved as independently as if she were simply walking. To Charles's credit, he kept her pace.

"Will you be visiting your family for the holiday?" Maggie asked as they turned.

"Unfortunately, my work has kept me here," Charles said. "My parents and brother are celebrating in Scotland with some of my mother's family there. But I couldn't manage the crossing this year."

"It was good of you to come tonight," Maggie said. "It is no good to be lonely this time of year."

Charles smirked. "I cannot say that was my motivation."

"Intriguing. Why, then, are you here if not for merrymaking?"

"I made some inquiries," Charles began, "...and I thought I might find you here."

"You came here to look for me?" Maggie asked incredulously. "You are aware of where I live."

"Well," Charles said slowly, buying himself time to gather his excuse, no doubt. "I thought to show up at your home would be obtrusive, and I was not sure if I would be allowed entry."

Maggie sank. "You've spoken with Walter," she concluded.

He nodded. "I figured that if there was a chance encounter on neutral ground..."

She quietly nodded, tears budding in her eyes for the third, or perhaps fourth, time in a single evening. "I'll have to meet with him, apologise if he will even have it."

The dance had ended, and Charles escorted her to the side before the next began.

"I am sure he will," Charles said earnestly as Maggie dabbed her eyes. Enough really was enough.

"Margaret!" Jonathan's unmistakable hiss sounded behind her.

Maggie turned slowly to face him. He was alone, jaw set in anger. "Where have you-" his question was cut short as his eyes flicked to Charles at her side. He straightened several inches, narrowed his eyes, and parted his lips much like a snarling animal. "What are you doing here?"

"Enjoying the festivities in your sister's delightful company," Charles said with a straight face and an even temper.

Jonathan looked down at her. "Have you been crying?" His attention snapped back to Charles. "You are truly a cad to enjoy torturing a woman this way," he growled.

"Jonathan," Maggie whispered sharply.

He lowered his tone to a dangerous whisper but showed no other sign of hearing her. "Do you have any idea what you have put her through already? I will not have you upset her again, not when-" Jonathan took a stiff breath. "You will do well to remove yourself from our company, sir."

"I will leave the moment the lady tells me so," Charles said, his tone set in such politeness to grate on Jonathan's last frayed nerve.

"She doesn't know what's good for her, clearly. I won't have you preying on her. Maggie, come at once," Jonathan said, taking her hand insistently.

"Jonathan, enough!" Maggie snapped, and he released her, looking back in shock that she would disobey him so publicly. In fact, a few of the partygoers had turned at this point to watch the unfolding scandal. The gentlemen both resumed a more dignified stance until they carried on, certainly with a gossip worthy story to spread. At last, she continued, "Jonathan, I am capable of caring for myself. As I have told you many times, Charles has done nothing to earn this loathing of yours. He is blameless in this."

Jonathan said nothing, grinding his teeth almost audibly. Just then, Camila emerged from the crowd beaming. Her eyes flickered between Jonathan and Charles, noting their distinctly unamused expressions.

"Jonathan, dear, I thought I had lost you," Camila said, linking her arm around his own. "I see you found Maggie." Her gaze shifted from Jonathan to her. "We were coming to find you to tell you the most splendid news."

She reached out her hand and displayed the ring, an eye catching oval cut emerald on a golden setting, which Maggie had helped Jonathan select two days before.

"It's so lovely, Camila," Maggie said. "I am so happy to bring you into the family."

"My congratulations to you both," Charles said, nodding.

Jonathan's narrowed eyes shot to him as Camila thanked him gracefully.

"We should return home," Jonathan said stiffly.

"But it's not yet midnight," Camila protested. "We simply must stay until then. It would be terribly rude."

"Terribly," Maggie repeated teasingly, despite herself.

Jonathan looked between Camila and Maggie, the struggle behind his eyes so evident Maggie almost pitied him.

"Come dance, Jonathan," Camila said softly and began to guide him toward the dance floor.

"A commendable brother you have there," Charles said under his breath.

"He really is," Maggie said earnestly. "Full of all the best intentions."

CHAPTER

12

"I'LL TAKE TEA IN MY parlor today," Maggie said, peeking into the kitchen. "Set for two."

The housekeeper gave her a sideways glance as her hands continued to chop the vegetables at a rather alarming speed. "Expecting that Mr. Davies?"

"Yes, Walter said he would be here at the half hour," Maggie said.

"I'll bring up a tray at quarter till," Mrs. Doyle said plainly. She set down her knife and turned fully, looking Maggie over for a moment. "At least you're dressing now," she concluded before turning back to the carrots.

Maggie rolled her eyes as she ducked out of the kitchen. It wasn't exactly a feat to manage a simple blouse and skirt. She'd tied her own hair that morning, employing a simple loose bun allowing her curls to fall as they would free of pins. Her mind was still fuming over how the good housekeeper would never comment on her dear brother that way when she nearly collided into him.

"Goodness, Maggie," Jonathan said. "Are you alright?"

"Yes," Maggie answered shortly.

"Well, I think that it's good that you and old Walter are making up," Jonathan said casually.

"Does everyone in this house feel the need to comment on my life as if it was a damned horse race?"

"Hardly, sister, your life is much more interesting," Jonathan said, positively beaming at his own cleverness. "I've been trying to get Mrs. Doyle in on some betting, but no luck as of yet."

"I will be upstairs," Maggie said pointedly as she skirted around him and made for the upstairs parlor.

When she came to the top of the stairs, Maggie let out a slow breath before she reached for the doorknob and turned it slowly. Her parlor was waiting within. She lingered in the doorway with a smile playing on her lips. It was not at all like it had been the last time she had entered here. There was no sense of foreboding lingering in the shadows nor fear quickening in her heart. This was a homecoming.

Maggie breathed in the scent of her incense. Her fingers traced over the soften leather bindings of her books. She smiled up at her bizarre crows who had such a fond place in her heart. Her eyes fell over the wardrobe and down to her seat. It was only then, as the mist touched her skin, that apprehension took root in her mind. For a long moment, she stood frozen. Was she truly ready for this?

A soft knock at the door freed her. Maggie was in motion at once, fueled by anxious energy. Walter stood on the other side, wearing his usual brown suit and wire glasses. He carried his doctor's bag and wore a hand knitted scarf around his neck. It was all so familiar, Maggie fought the urge to wrap him in a hug then and there.

Instead, she said a simple "Thank you for coming. You're rather earlier than I expected."

Walter took a step inside. "I may have been eager. I was not sure if I would hear from you again," he said.

"You have all my apologies, of course," Maggie said, feeling as though she might catch fire from the shame of it. "I was so horrible. There's absolutely no excuse. After everything-" she shook her head.

"After everything, I daresay your reaction was not outside the realm of reason," Walter conceded. "I admit the events were truly shaking to the sanity from my own perspective. I can imagine whatever you experienced was a good deal more troubling, to say the least."

Maggie shook her head.

"I was hoping that I might interview you on the experience, if you are able," Walter said. "I believe speaking about it may help bring you some peace."

"I-" she hesitated but bolstered herself and pushed on. "Yes, I am able, if you like."

"I will set up then," Walter said, pulling out his recording device and setting it on the table. "I must say that this case has been playing on my mind these past weeks. I've been researching extensively. I have many thoughts which I would like to share with you, but first, I require the final piece, you understand."

"Of course," Maggie said, taking a seat and forcing an even breath.

"I am glad you reached out. I've been preparing to make a second expedition, if you will, but I think to venture there alone would be... ill advised."

"I would say so," Maggie said grimly.

"There we are," Walter said triumphantly as he finished his preparations. "Shall we?"

Maggie nodded.

The needle began to scratch against the record.

"Hello, the date is December 28th, 1916, and I, Walter Davies of the ASPR, am here with medium Maggie Barlow to discuss her account of the events of November 26th."

"Where shall I begin?" Maggie asked, smoothing her skirt.

"When did you first feel a spiritual presence in the house?"

"Not until we were seated, until I began searching for it," Maggie began. "Ordinarily in a sitting, I will seek out a spirit by name, prompted by my clients. In this case, of course, the spirit's identity is unknown. Yet, almost immediately, I could feel its presence as though it were near. I had not experienced that before."

Walter nodded, looking at his notebook. "At the time, you commented that it was very cold. My devices noticed only a small flux in the temperature throughout the duration of the sitting."

Maggie shuffled. "Whenever I reach out, there is a sensation of coldness which I have grown used to. But in that house... the chill was closer than usual, and more intense."

"And then?"

"I tried to establish a connection, but it was eluding me consciously. They don't usually..."

"I see. It was very responsive, however. The knocking, the scratchings into the table."

"Yes."

Walter paused. "And then you cried out."

The needle scratched on the record, and Maggie shut her eyes tightly, trying to keep that wretched memory from gripping her again.

"Take your time."

Maggie nodded. "I connected with the spirit." She scoffed. "It connected with me, pulled me... To make any connection, I have to venture into the dark where they lie, like wading ankle deep into a freezing ocean to see the fish. But this... the spirit pulled me under. It was nothing but darkness and cold where nothing could live. I couldn't live. And I felt its anger. I saw it killing Anne..." Her voice choked as a chill passed up her spine. Maggie took a shuddering breath and pressed on. "I saw it attacking Ruthie. I thought it was going to kill me too."

"But it did not," Walter said firmly.

"No, it didn't," Maggie agreed.

"My last question: How did you manage to free yourself?"

She straightened, collecting herself. "I reminded myself that I was alive."

Walter nodded approvingly and took the needle off the record. He let out a heavy breath as he sat back down and began to clean his glasses thoughtfully. They sat in mindful silence for several moments before Walter fixed them on his nose and cleared his throat.

"As I told you before, in the past weeks, I have done a depth of research into the subject, combining it with my own experiences. I suppose I was coping in my own scientific manner." He paused to rub his chin. "I have come upon a theory, one which I wanted your personal testimony to corroborate."

"And has it?"

"Well, yes. I do believe so," Walter said in wonderment.

"Well, don't leave me in suspense," Maggie teased weakly.

"Hardly," Walter said, straightening himself with a small smile. "Where to begin..." He fumbled for a moment. "I don't suppose you might have some spare paper?"

"Of course, I keep some for writings." Maggie stood at once and retrieved some from the drawer in the old sewing table, a carryover from her youth now serving a better purpose, storing odds and ends for her practice.

"Naturally, thank you," Walter said as he took out a pencil.

"Right then. So I shall begin, and do stop me if I become too complex to follow. The first principle of my theory involves two parallel and constant states of being." He drew a long line on the paper and then another below. "The first is one with which you are very familiar, the material plane. As the name suggests, this plane contains all matter."

"Matter of what?" Maggie asked, already lost.

"Matter, yes, you see, all things around us are made of atoms, either in solid, liquid, or gaseous state."

"Yes, of course."

"Matter is the term to describe anything that contains atoms and therefore has mass."

"So you say that the material plane contains all matter, but matter is everything, so what could possibly be left?" Maggie asked, brow furrowed.

"Well, no, matter only describes what has mass. Allow me to continue. I think you may follow." Maggie nodded obligingly. "Yes, so the material plane contains all matter. Matter, or rather the consumption of it, is required to produce light, heat, and of course, life. None of these things I have just listed have mass and are therefore not matter, yet they also exist only on this plane." He redrew the top line in emphasis.

Maggie nodded for him to continue, fingers pressed against her lips in concentration.

"Secondarily, this plane, which I have taken to call the Nether plane, or the lower, if you will, contains what is essentially the defaulted state of the universe. It is the substantial absence of matter, light, and heat. Thus, this plane of being contains nothing but darkness and cold."

Maggie dropped her hands, green eyes staring at him widely.

"I can see you are drawing conclusions," Walter said. His blue eyes simmered with controlled excitement. "Allow me to continue, and we shall see if we have arrived at the same place."

Maggie nodded quickly.

"So we see the interactions between these two planes of being constantly. When there is no source of heat, it is cold. When there is no light, it is dark."

"Yes."

"Right, so how is this relevant to our purposes? I believe you may already have an idea. When a body dies, when a person no longer has mass and energy, or you might say life, they die, but what if, as spiritualism suggests, the spirit lives on? I believe that it does. I believe that it falls to the Nether and continues on."

Maggie could feel her skin begin to prick as if with a chill.

"I theorise that these spirits have varying levels of awareness of the material world, and most lose connection with it completely and simply exist in this void. However, it is the others that concern our work together. I believe that some spirits manage to reach briefly across this divide and affect matter on the material plane. Now your analogy, of icy water, that is, is a perfect illustration. Picture this frigid water and the fish within. I would say that what we witnessed that night were splashes, if you will."

"But how?" Maggie asked.

Walter sighed. "I haven't the slightest clue. Perhaps it is simply a matter of will."

Maggie sat for a moment. "This is truly fascinating, Walter, but I really don't see how this can help us."

"As to that!" Walter said enthusiastically, digging through his bag. "I found an account from a psychic in Scotland only a few decades ago. I made note of it. Your testimony is highly similar to what Ms. Hughes describes. Ah, here!" He pulled out one of his small journals and opened it to the marked page.

"And I shall not allow any spirit to pull me from the land of the living, from my mortal body, and into their dark beyond, else I would risk losing my way. I tie myself to the lifeblood of another, feel their ardent hearts at work as I reach across the divide. Thus, I can draw them to myself so that they might speak, and I shall hear."

"She speaks as though she does not cross the barrier," Maggie contemplated.

"Her writings seem to suggest that it is a dangerous undertaking to do so. Perhaps that is the nature of the tradition of clasping hands during a sitting, to ground the psychic for such a purpose."

"I had never thought," Maggie said. "God, I've been so reckless. I should have-"

"Did you have any training as a medium before you began for yourself?"

Maggie shook her head. "I've practiced on my own for years, in some capacity or another, but I've never met another like myself."

"I see," Walter said. "Then you can hardly blame yourself when you have learned only from self discovery. Now I have a question, how young were you when you first experienced a sense of the Nether?"

"That is difficult to say," Maggie answered. "I've felt whispers since I was a girl. I always thought I was imagining. But as I grew older, they continued. I was seventeen when I was sure that it was not all in my own mind."

"When you were a child, did you have any serious illness or near death experiences?"

"No, I was a very healthy child. I've never even broken a bone."

"Tea?" They both turned to see Jonathan standing in the doorway with the tea tray.

"Since when do you bring the tea?" Maggie nearly laughed at the thought.

"My ledgers were hardly good company today. I hope I'm not intruding?"

"I suppose not," Maggie said, looking to Walter who confirmed the same.

Jonathan sat as Maggie began to fix her tea with two sugars.

"You know, you were wrong before," Jonathan said, biting into a biscuit.

"What?" Maggie asked in surprise.

"Is that so?" Walter asked, taking out his notebook.

"Well," Jonathan shuffled under their sudden vamped interest. "When Maggie was four or five, I can't recall, she was climbing a tree. She fell from a low branch. In the moment, it didn't seem like a terrible fall, but she lost consciousness. She was unwell for the whole day, very unwell." He shuffled again, like a nervous child. "A doctor was called at once, of course, but he couldn't stop the seizures. There was... Well I heard him speaking to Mother that she might not survive the night." He swallowed hard and let out a humorless laugh. "Didn't sleep a wink that night, but it must have done the trick because you were right as rain the next day. Nanny wouldn't let you out of the nursery for a week. You were nearly climbing the curtains by the end."

"How have I never heard this story?" Maggie asked, still hardly able to believe it.

"Well, Mother and Father are hardly ones to reminisce, especially about something so... unpleasant."

"You'd be amazed how many mediums have had similar experiences," Walter said.

"Really?" Jonathan inquired.

"Oh yes."

"So, you really think that Maggie has some... talent?" Jonathan asked.

"Without doubt," Walter said, nodding. "What I witnessed at the Blackbourne house was undeniable."

Jonathan's posture changed so quickly that Walter said no more. Her brother looked at her with heavy brows and leaned back in his seat, crossing his fingers. "Mr. Blackbourne is a client," Jonathan repeated her words.

"I told you," Maggie said stubbornly.

"Why at his home?" Jonathan asked, this time turning to Walter.

"Well, unlike many other clients who simply wish to contact the deceased, Mr. Blackbourne was experiencing spiritual disturbances in his home."

"You were there because his house is haunted?" Jonathan said disbelievingly, turning back to her. He sighed and rubbed his face. "Good God, Maggie. And you came back- What the hell happened there?"

Maggie opened her mouth, unsure what even to say, when Walter spoke instead.

"I would spare her to relive it again. It is simple enough to say that there is truly something horrible in that house, and your sister faced it very bravely."

Maggie scoffed. To describe any of her actions of late as brave seemed a cruel misuse of the word.

"You've been upset all these weeks because you saw a ghost?" Jonathan asked her. God, it sounded so childish.

"If you're going to-" Maggie started hotly.

"No-" Jonathan said. "Forgive me. I've misjudged this situation greatly. You can hardly blame me though. The truth is stranger than fiction, for Christ's sake." He rubbed his jaw for a moment. "So what now? You must be up here plotting to do something about it, I suppose."

"You actually believe me?" Maggie questioned.

"Oh, certainly not," Jonathan said easily. "But you all seem to, and the sooner this is done with the better, I think? So how does one remove a ghost?"

"I've just come to clear, sir," Mrs. Doyle huffed from the doorway. "I hope your sister is not roping you into her wickedness."

"Not to worry." Jonathan smiled at her winningly.

"The only people who should be dealing with unholy spirits are the lord's men. You two shouldn't be trifling the way you are!"

"An exorcism!" Maggie exclaimed, startling everyone. "Do you think it would actually work?"

"It's possible, I suppose," Walter said. "There certainly are accounts of-"

"Of all the things, only a priest can perform the holy rites," Mrs. Doyle protested.

"Do you know one?" Maggie asked.

"You two can't be serious?" Jonathan interrupted.

"If you are going to do this properly, I can talk to my cousin, Father Duncan," Mrs. Doyle said seriously. "He'll sort this mess out."

"You can't waste the poor man's time," Jonathan continued, ignored.

"Mrs. Doyle, that would be wonderful!" Maggie said.

"I could set an appointment," Walter offered.

Mrs. Doyle huffed begrudgingly, but her discontent did nothing to dampen Maggie's renewed spirit.

"You two don't seriously mean to go back there?" Jonathan asked.

"What's the matter?" Maggie asked. "I thought you didn't believe in ghosts?"

CHAPTER

13

FATHER DUNCAN TURNED the corner to see three figures awaiting him just beyond the threshold of the house. Even in the dark, he knew who they must be. The night was far too cold for loitering in such a way. As he drew nearer, he recognised the man and woman who had come into his offices with the most unusual request. Mr. Davies was reading from a small notebook scrawled with writings which he murmured to himself as he turned the pages. Resting on the step beside him was a doctor's case. Ms. Barlow turned up to meet him. She seemed far too young, and admittedly too pretty, to be wrapped up in such unsettling business. The third, a man with dark hair and eyes to match, had his arm wrapped around her for warmth.

He must be the widower. A moment of condemnation passed over him as their touch showed a certain sort of familiarity.

However, he pushed the thought away. No man can grieve forever, and even so, his judgement rested with the Holy Father alone.

"Father Duncan!" Maggie greeted as the trio turned to face him. In the dim luminescence of the lamp light, the oil in his brown hair reflected brightly as his black Cossack suit blended into the surrounding darkness. "I am so pleased that you came."

"I have," Father Duncan said slowly, "as a favor to my dear cousin and to hopefully put your minds at rest."

"This is Mr. Blackbourne, the owner of the house," Maggie introduced.

"My condolences for your loss," he said as they shook. "As I said, I do believe that people often scare themselves with these matters of spiritualism. True occurrences are very rare."

Maggie and Walter exchanged a brief look.

"We are happy to have your expertise all the same," Walter said diplomatically.

"As I said in our meeting, this is not a sanctioned exorcism as it has not been approved by the bishop," Father Duncan explained. "Thus being, there are limits to what I can do here tonight."

"We understand, Father," Maggie said. "We are all very grateful for your help all the same."

Father Duncan nodded.

"Before we enter, I've prepared the sacraments for us to take in the Holy Communion."

They stood, rather bizarrely, in the street as Father Duncan offered the bread and wine to each of them, offering the blessings as Christ had done long ago. When it was finished, they turned to the house.

In the darkness, it loomed over them as if it did not want to be entered at all. Though it was not truly the shadow of the house which brought the sensation of foreboding, but her knowledge of what dwelt within. Charles led them up the steps, his manner determinedly stoic. The key turned in the lock, and the door slowly swung open like a gaping demon's mouth, revealing the cavernous dark within.

"I had the electrics shut off," Charles said, not turning, eyes fixed into the hall of his former home.

"Not to worry," Walter said. "I've brought portable lights."

He handed one to Maggie and the other to Charles before equipping himself with his electrical measuring device. Charles took the first steps into the hall, followed closely by the Father and Maggie, with Walter taking the rear. It was clear even in the dark that all was not how it had been left weeks ago.

"Merciful God," Father Duncan whispered as the lights moved across every ruined detail.

Every mirror or vase was shattered, every painting or portrait torn. The furnishings were scattered and broken across the floor. The draperies had been shredded as if by monstrous claws, the work of which could be seen on the wooden floors and across the wallpaper as well. But what drew the eyes of each of the four was written on every surface, high and low, *murder, murder, murder.* The word surrounded them.

"In the name of the Father, and of the Son, and of the Holy Ghost. Amen," Father Duncan began to mutter, an ominous overture to all they saw before them. "Most glorious Prince of the Heavenly Armies, Saint Michael the Archangel, defend us in our battle against principalities and powers, against the rulers of this world of darkness, against the spirits of wickedness in the high places..."

Maggie's hands shook as she stepped over the cursed threshold once more. Not shook, they shivered. It was cold within the house, colder than it had been just before standing in the snow. Maggie felt it surround her so overwhelmingly that she nearly lost her footing.

"Maggie!" Walter said, steadying her.

She gripped his arm tightly, remembering what he had read to her. *I tie myself to the lifeblood of another.* Maggie could feel it, his life, warm, insistent. She felt the same sensation grow within her own body. Soon her mind cleared. Still, the icy sensation surrounded her, but she found it tolerable enough to continue on. They had all stopped in silence, all but the priest who never ceased uttering his prayer. Maggie nodded for them to carry on.

"In here," Charles said, directing them to the sitting room. "I'll light a fire."

They all entered behind him, senses keen for the slightest noise to bring them to alert. The mantle sprung to life with flames that grew to cast their shadows across the wall, flickering in a distorted dance.

"The temperature grows colder deeper within the house," Walter observed.

"I feel it," Maggie said simply. The words seemed such an understatement as her breaths shuddered. It was as if she was a single candle in the snow.

Maggie steeled herself as the priest continued. "In the name of Jesus Christ, our God and Lord, strengthened by the intercession of the Immaculate Virgin Mary, Mother of God-"

Father Duncan's speech stumbled as something shattered on the second floor overhead. Maggie's flashlight turned instinctively toward the noise, falling on the ruined remains of Anne's piano sitting lifeless and silent against the wall.

"...of Blessed Michael the Archangel-"

A heavy THUMP sounded from the floor above.

"Maggie?" Charles breathed as he came to stand at her side.

Father Duncan began again slowly, "...of the Blessed Apostles Peter and Paul and all the Saints."

Charles's hand gripped her arm as a horrible scratching like that of talons carving into wood began to descend the stairs. Walter's device sparked wildly, the light reflecting in his spectacles.

Maggie could feel her heart beating and her mouth go dry. Walter stared about wide eyed as Charles held the portable light out into the darkness of the hallway. Father Duncan continued to read from his book with a greater resolve. It was clear upon his face that any doubts he once held had melted wholly away.

"We confidently undertake to repulse the attacks and deceits of the devil. God arises; His enemies are scattered, and those who hate Him flee before Him. As smoke is driven away, so are they driven; as wax melts before the fire, so the wicked perish at the presence of God."

As he finished, the phantom scratchings reached the bottom of the stairs and stopped, leaving them in a silence filled with tangible dread. Maggie did not need to reach out her senses. The veil was upon this place like a frigid mist against her skin. The spirit was drifting just on the boundary, stalking like a tiger looking for a weak point to allow it passage through completely. Maggie could feel its longing, its furious desire to escape, a consuming clawing ache.

The quiet lasted only a moment before Father Duncan read valiantly on. "We drive you from us, whoever you may be, unclean spirits, all satanic powers, all infernal invaders, all wicked legion-"

What he said next was drowned by a sudden piercing shriek, so resounding each of them could not help but cover their ears, though it offered no relief. Maggie felt herself sinking to her knees, Charles pressed at her side. By the light of the fire, Maggie saw through her watering eyes as Father Duncan was lifted as if by an invisible noose many inches off the ground. It was hard to make out at first, but his book of prayers was there before him, no longer in his hands. Though the sound was lost amongst the screaming, Maggie saw the pages being torn savagely in the air, the mangled bits falling to the ground below his feet.

The spirit's presence was growing. It had seeded itself deeply in this place. Maggie could feel it pushing against the barrier. Instinct overcame her, a power stirred, and Maggie pushed back. At once, she felt warmer, a candle grown into a flame. Maggie looked to Walter and Charles, who had fallen to the floor, their eyes fixed on the priest held brutally over the ground in utter horror. Father Duncan seemed unable to move in any way, even to form words, but they could hear the noises of terror sounding in his throat.

As Maggie found her own ability swell, the ringing in her ears grew dull. She pulled herself to her feet. As if in response, the horrid cry began to change into a low, rumbling growl.

"Get out!" it said in a voice like a bark. Maggie did not know if the others had heard. Yet, they all watched wide eyed as Father Duncan was thrown across the room into the mangled remains of the piano which let out a defeated cord as his body fell.

He crumpled to the floor, motionless. Charles and Maggie ran to him, Charles reaching him first.

"He's alive," Charles said.

"Maggie!" Walter called.

He was standing in the center of the room, looking up. Into the molding of the ceiling, a new message was carved, *M... A... G...* Her name stared back at her, scrawled into the plaster. Maggie's stomach twisted as if she would be sick. All at once, she felt terribly small and utterly frightened.

"This has gone too far! We must leave now!" Charles said, taking her by the hand.

Before any protest could be made or action taken, the drawing doors slammed themselves shut, blocking their exit. Walter tested them, rattling the oak within its frame to no avail. Charles released her as he went to help. Maggie looked around at the destruction, the men's frantic attempts to free their escape, Father Duncan's unconscious body, her name on the ceiling. In the corners of her perception, the spirit prowled still.

The fear inside her raged so terribly her blood turned to ice, so terribly she couldn't stand it. It twisted in her chest, transforming even as she thought her heart would burst.

"You!" Maggie called out in a furious cry. "Leave this place!" A chair in the corner began to rattle and shake, followed by an end table that was upside down by the wall. "You do not belong here!"

"Maggie!" Charles called out desperately.

She whirled around to see the chair flying toward her. As if by some other will than her own, Maggie raised up her hand, and it clattered suddenly to the floor and lay still.

"That is enough!" Maggie rebuked fiercely. "You will haunt this place no longer!"

And at last, Maggie caught it in her sights. For the first time, she saw the spirit plain as she made the connection at last.

But it was not at all like in the past when she was gripped and pulled into that horrible abyss. They met on the boundary. Maggie could feel her body, see the ruined room around them. But still, the spirit was all around her, their consciousnesses joined.

It was fury and longing, but it was something else that sent her to her knees, an utterly broken heart.

"Maggie!" Charles turned from the door and rushed to her side.

Maggie could not answer for the tears pouring from her eyes, tears not her own. His attention snapped as the doors to the kitchen flew open.

"Charles," a soft and mournful voice called out.

His eyes widened as he looked down through the kitchen. The garden door had been thrown open as well. Beyond, she stood on the snow covered cobblestones of the garden, and Maggie could see through her eyes as Charles's grew wide.

"Anne?" he said disbelievingly.

"Don't leave me again," Anne sobbed. Her words echoed in Maggie's mind a second before they were spoken, or perhaps she just knew what she would say. They were joined in every way. She was losing herself between two minds, two bodies. The connection had become so tangled, she couldn't get free.

"Maggie, are you with us?" Walter whispered, touching her shoulder.

For a second, she was back to herself but still could not manage to speak because it was Anne's words that played in her mind. "I love you, Charles."

Charles stood slowly, trance like. Maggie reached for him desperately. He couldn't go to her. Maggie could see her mind. They could not stay here, not a moment more. But Maggie's hand didn't move, not an inch. It was Anne's. Her graceful arm stretched out, beckoning him in.

"No!" Maggie's scream came as a whisper, but it was enough.

"Charles, stop!" Walter called out, going to his feet at once.

"That's my- my wife! She's-" Charles's voice was thick and choked.

"Charles!" The voice cried out painfully. Tears began to roll freely down Charles's face.

"No!" Maggie commanded, still unable to find her own feet.

Anne's anger flared, crippling her as the fire beneath the mantle surged forth into the room, causing many pieces of furniture and other debris to be caught in the flames, as well as Walter's coat. Perhaps the shock had disentangled her, but Maggie found herself rushing to help him remove the flaming garment. Maggie's eyes watered from the smoke as the fire spread rapidly. Charles was standing motionless, staring at the door leading to the kitchen. Though she could no longer see her, Maggie knew that Anne continued her vigil in that cursed garden.

"Charles!" Maggie called through a fit of coughing. He did not turn but instead disappeared, dashing through the doorway. "Get Father Duncan out of here!" Maggie yelled to Walter as she raced after Charles as best she could, avoiding the growing flames.

Maggie heard Walter call after her, but she did not slow. She entered the kitchen, but Charles was no longer there. The garden door was closed, and Maggie knew that he was on the other side, with her.

Yet, as Maggie had reclaimed her own body, her awareness of Anne's had fallen away. The fear mounted within her. "Charles!" Maggie cried again.

She reached out her mind, searching for Charles through Anne's eyes. It was easily done, the stepping between minds. There Charles was, the winter winds whipping through his dark hair as he looked back at her. Not her, Anne.

"I lost you- How..?" he said. His eyes were wide and broken.

Maggie could not mourn for him as she wished, not as she saw into Anne's thoughts, what she meant now to do.

She ripped her consciousness free, only realizing what was about to transpire moments before catastrophe struck. Each of the stove knobs had been turned to release the gas. Heart racing, head spinning, Maggie darted into the maid's room and slammed the door shut behind her. However, this was all the time she had.

The blast blew the door from its hinges and sent Maggie colliding with the footboard of the brass bed frame. The door impacted her at the same moment. Intense heat billowed into the room heralded by plumes of searing smoke. The dark clouds filled the room and Maggie's lungs as she coughed profusely. Her head spun though still, she found the strength to remove the door from her back. She covered her mouth with the skirt of her dress, crawling to the corner of the room. Thankfully it had not caught fire. Maggie took the end table which lay discarded on its side and slammed it against the window with all her remaining might.

Fresh air flowed freely into her lungs again as Maggie stuck her head from the window. The explosion had damaged the back wall of the kitchen, leaving its debris scattered throughout the garden. Charles lay against the farthest brick wall now alone. Maggie reached out her senses, looking for Anne as she used the end table to knock away the glass. They were no longer connected. Perhaps the blast had shaken it loose. Past the terror, Maggie could feel nothing else. She took the thick blanket from the bed and placed it over the windowsill. With effort, she climbed out into the garden and dashed over to where Charles lay, tripping over the many loose stones.

He was lying still at an awkward angle, head bleeding into the snow.

"Wake up!" Maggie said desperately as she fell to his side.

She shook his shoulder desperately, shouting his name through her burning throat. He stirred slowly, but as he saw the house behind her billowing with smoke, Charles quickly attempted to get to his feet. His balance was unsteady. Maggie supported as much of his weight as she could until he found his footing. They were surrounded on three sides by solid brick, leaving their only escape through the flaming house. The kitchen wall had been destroyed, and Maggie could see a possible path through the kitchen to the hall. Charles saw the same. Wrapping the blanket around them, he led her at a fast pace back into the house.

The heat was unbearable, but as they left the fire climbing the walls of the kitchen, it had not spread to the hall, save for a few testing licks of flame. They hunched low in the blanket, coughing and covering their mouths from the smoke as they darted down that hall.

The front door was open before them, the wintry winds just beyond. Only feet from the threshold, as they passed the blazing doors of the sitting room, they burst open. A surge of heat like hell blasted into their faces and splatters of liquid fire ignited the blanket. They could not help but shield themselves with their arms helplessly against the inferno.

And in this moment, she pounced, latching onto Maggie once more, sinking her claws deep and pulling herself up from the darkness.

"Charles!" Anne's voice cried out. "Don't leave me, Charles."

She stood in the center of the room, consumed by the flames, pleading. This was what she wanted. Not to be alone in that nothingness, not any longer.

"Charles, you can't," Maggie pleaded, fighting for every word as Charles hesitated, stunned by the sight of her.

The door was open only feet away. Maggie could see the promise of fresh, cool air.

"Charles!" Maggie said, pulling him back to reality. "We'll die in here!"

Charles did not look back at her. He could not, frozen in grief and shock, crippled by a broken heart. The only way to save him was to bring this to an end.

Maggie pulled and clawed and fought, digging Anne from her mind like a weed from a garden. Her grip was determined, desperate. Maggie used every ounce of her will as her roots dug in, grasping for purchase.

"No more!" Maggie strained with the last of her strength. A faint feeling came over her as at last she was free. Her balance was unsteady, weak.

Anne's figure lingered for a moment. Though Maggie could no longer feel her presence within her, she knew that Anne's spirit could not linger now, not here. Through the heat and smoke and flame, she was lost as vapor.

"Charles," Maggie forced through her searing throat. "Please."

He gazed bewildered into the flames for a moment longer before his dark eyes met her own wide with realization.

Without reply, Charles scooped Maggie up in his arms and crossed the threshold of the house out into the street. Walter met them on the third step as Maggie's lungs begged for the fresh air.

Before a word between them could be uttered, a tremendous crash ripped through the air as glass shattered, raining down shards from overhead. The house burst into flames, escaping through each of the windows and allowing the smoke to trail freely into the night.

Maggie glimpsed the flame, the smoke, the stars of the winter sky, and then she went slack in Charles's arms.

CHAPTER

14

MURDER, MURDER, MURDER.

Consciousness crashed into Maggie, sending her bolt upright in the unfamiliar bed. White sheets covered her body. White curtains hung from metal frames surrounding the bed, hiding her view of anything beyond. Against them, Camila's dark blue coat was a foreign splash of color.

"Oh, Maggie! You're alright," Camila said, standing at once and coming to her side. "Jonathan!" she called, glancing over her shoulder. "He's just gone off for a moment. He'll be back soon."

Where's Charles? Maggie meant to ask. Instead, she managed only "Wh-" before a terrible searing pain inflamed her throat and sent her into a fit of even more torturous coughs.

"Hold on!" Camila said, turning to the pitcher on her bedside and filling a glass with water.

As Maggie reached for the glass, every movement made her skin itch and burn. Maggie could not help but gasp sharply at the sensation. Her arms were wrapped in bandages from her hand nearly to her shoulders. She could bend her elbows and flex her fingers, though they were all wrapped together in thick bandage mittens.

"It's alright," Camila said, voice steady. "The doctor said they were only minor burns from heat exposure. Oh, Maggie, we were so worried. They said it was an accident with the gas line. It brought the whole house down. It's a miracle you all survived. Here, drink this."

Maggie nodded, and Camila helped her drain the entire glass and then a second. Only then did she try her voice again.

She sounded as though she had been screaming for hours. "Where is Charles?"

Camila shuffled uncomfortably. "He's gone to his apartment, I think. He came to visit, but Jonathan thought it wasn't for the best."

Maggie shut her eyes as her mind raced. No, no, no. "I need to see him now. It can't wait," Maggie insisted, sitting up in bed fully despite the pain.

"Maggie, you really can't go," Camila said.

It was then that Jonathan emerged from behind the curtain with Walter in tow.

"Maggie!" Jonathan said with great relief. "Thank goodness. I've just spoken with the doctor, and he said that you could return home as soon as you were awake. We can look after you there."

"She says that it is urgent that she leave to see Charles," Camila said.

Maggie looked at her, gaping, feeling terribly betrayed.

"What?" Jonathan exclaimed, going pale.

"Maggie, really, you must recover," Walter added. His suit coat was still blackened where it had been burnt by the flames.

"You are trying to put me in an early grave," Jonathan said, finding his voice. "Not only do I get a call from the hospital of all things- worried absolutely sick- You've been unconscious for hours- You can't go wandering the streets! For the sake of my sanity, would you please be reasonable for twenty four hours! My nerves-" He exhaled violently as Camila set a gentle hand on his arm.

"Your brother is absolutely right," Camila said firmly.

"It's Charles," Maggie rasped. "He's in danger. I have to-"

"Maggie, please, you've been through an ordeal," Camila said.

"Mr. Blackbourne is entirely well at his apartment," Jonathan growled.

"I saw him myself," Walter agreed. "His burns were treated, and his head injury was fairly minor. The doctor released him some hours ago. Father Duncan will need a few more days to recover, but-"

Maggie shook her head violently. "It was Anne. It was her all along."

"What?" Walter's brows raised as Camila looked at her in concern.

"Who the hell is Anne? Walter, what is she talking about?" Jonathan demanded.

"Jonathan, don't curse," Camila said.

"I saw her," Maggie confirmed.

"I see," Walter said slowly, "but it is over now. I promise. The house is totally destroyed-"

"Murder," Maggie managed desperately through her ruined throat. "She told us again and again. Someone killed her, Walter!"

"Dear god," Walter said, removing his glasses.

"Would you please tell me what is going on!" Jonathan demanded, having well and truly reached the end of his tether.

"The maid," Walter said suddenly.

Maggie nodded. "She told us." Her mind went back to the first time she had seen that horrid word scratched above Ruthie's bed. She had been identifying her killer.

"You're saying that Mr. Blackbourne's maid killed someone?" Jonathan asked.

"She killed his wife," Walter said, replacing his glasses and standing straighter. "He's likely with her now."

Maggie pushed off her blankets and hissed as she discovered another burn stretching across her left side.

Jonathan was nearly purple and quite beyond words, therefore resorting to a spew of furious and illegible syllables.

"Jonathan," Maggie said, voice clearer now than it was when she woke, though still, it was gravely and hoarse. "He's in real danger. If you have any love for me at all, you will let me go."

171

"If you honestly think-" Jonathan huffed again. "You should be calling the police."

"To be frank," Walter said, "I hardly think it would do any good. We have no permissible evidence to link her to the crime."

Jonathan ran his fingers through his hair, looking rather murderous himself. "This is insanity," he hissed, but in such a way that they all could tell he had given in.

"I'll help you dress," Camila said at once. "I brought you some clothes."

Jonathan stood irritably for a moment, unwilling to completely abandon his objections, but soon he followed Walter's lead and left them be.

Maggie tried to change quickly, but there was simply no way to rush the process. Even though Camila had thoughtfully brought a simple dress that fastened easily in the front, it took far longer than she had hoped to ease into a garment suitable for the street. All the while, she could hear her brother's grumblings from behind the curtain.

Maggie emerged at last with a small smile, which was really more of a wince. Truthfully she was in a great deal of pain and would have gladly listened to her brother and stayed in bed for days if Charles's mortal well being was not hanging precariously in the balance.

Jonathan looked down at her grumpily but said nothing.

"Let's go!" Camila said.

"Surely you're not coming?" Maggie asked in surprise.

"Of course we are!" Jonathan snapped.

And there was nothing more said on the matter.

Walter hailed the cab and directed the car to the Chatsworth building where Charles had taken up residence. Maggie sat beside Camila, resting her head against the cold window. Her burns made even the smallest motion sear and itch, and every last bit of her ached. A large bruise on her forehead throbbed as it pulsed with blood. Maggie shut her eyes against the pain as the car began to move.

"Maggie?" Camila said, touching her shoulder as lightly as possible.

The cab had stopped. They were at the base of the Chatsworth. Maggie nodded sorely. She accepted Jonathan's careful help down from the car, which was difficult without the use of her arms.

"It's apartment twelve," Walter said, already racing quickly to the lobby.

Maggie was practically shaking as Walter spoke to the doorman, who at last pointed them to the elevator. She could only imagine how ragged they must have appeared, not to mention frantic. Not a part of her eased as they stepped onto the elevator or even out onto the third floor.

"Camila, please keep her here," Jonathan said as he approached door number twelve with furious long legged strides.

"What?" Maggie croaked furiously.

"You drag me here to confront a murderess. You could at least have the decency to heed me in this," Jonathan hissed.

"Perhaps-" Walter began, but then the door opened.

Ruthie stood on the other side, dressed in her black uniform. "You are here to see Mr. Charles?"

"Yes," Walter said, managing to overcome the shock first. "We heard about his ordeal and wanted to be sure he was well."

"He's in the parlor," she said, opening the door a little wider and standing out of the way.

"Thank you," Camila said. Though her voice was polite, Maggie could see that she was shaken.

It was as if all their hearts had merged into one thundering pulse as they entered the apartment. Though Maggie recognised none of the paintings, or other items decorating the hall, she could feel Charles's taste about them. He favored forest colors, dark grained woods, and hunting scenes. This was his place.

Ruthie walked ahead of them a short way to the first door. "Mr. Charles, visitors for you," she introduced them.

Charles was sitting heavily in a plush leather armchair before a hearty fire. He was without a jacket. The sleeves of his white shirt were rolled to his elbows. One of his forearms was wrapped in thick bandages. On the table beside him was a glass of scotch. Lily, his red and white hound, was resting at his feet. He looked tired. More than tired, he looked utterly wretched. He hardly lifted his head as they entered.

"Charles," Maggie said, coming to his side.

"I've just been making dinner. Shall I make enough for five?" Ruthie asked.

Charles shook his head in a hardly discernible way. Still she turned, whistling for the dog who came obediently trotting after her down the hall, leaving them.

"Maggie," Charles said. "I'm so sorry." Even as he looked at her, his brown eyes were dull, distant.

"Maggie," Jonathan whispered behind her urgently.

She slid her bandaged hand into Charles's and squeezed. His returned gesture was weak.

"Something's wrong," Maggie whispered, studying his vague features as he murmured another apology.

"We have to get him back to the hospital," Camila said, coming beside her.

"No," Ruthie's voice echoed and hung heavily over the parlor. She was standing in the doorway, a hunting rifle in her arms.

"Oh my god," Camila whispered, peddling back.

"What are you-" Charles stood to confront her but swayed for a moment.

The room called out as he fell. Maggie caught him as best she could, but his weight sent her tumbling, pinning her to the ground.

"Charles!" Maggie shrieked, trying to discern if he was still breathing. His chest rose gently atop her, though he was utterly unconscious.

"Get by the mantle!" Ruthie shouted, directing the rifle toward Walter and Jonathan.

"Set down the gun and-" Jonathan said in his best attempt at a calm yet stern command.

"You'll tell me nothing and do as I say," she growled. "You shouldn't have come. It wasn't supposed to be like this. It was supposed to be the two of us. Just us."

Maggie watched as Jonathan and Walter raised their arms and stepped toward the mantle. Beside her, Camila was staring up at her brother in a way that could break a heart. Ruthie positioned herself between them and their escape, attention moving between them frantically.

"You can walk away from this," Walter promised.

"No! Quiet," Ruthie said.

Maggie looked into her eyes. She was unhinged but calculating. There had been a plan for tonight, and it wasn't going right. The rifle had been prepared just in case. And in that moment, a horrific realization came to her; this was not a desperate attempt to escape from her crimes. Ruthie had no intention of living through this night, and she was willing to take them all with her.

"It was just supposed to be us, for once, just us," Ruthie muttered to herself. Suddenly her focus turned to Maggie. "This is all because of you. This is all your fault! I've loved him since I was a girl. I know him. Not you..."

Maggie forced herself not to look into the barrel of the gun though she felt it watching her like a black, sightless eye.

Ruthie nodded to herself even as tears rolled down her cheeks. "He would have seen me... He would have chosen me, if it wasn't for you. None of this..." Her eyes fell to him, limp on the carpet as her voice broke. "None of this would have had to happen. None of it..."

A shiver ran down Maggie's spine. Only feet from the fire, she shivered, and not from fear. It was cold, freezing. "Anne," Maggie whispered.

"Don't say her name!" Ruthie's voice was between a growl and a sob.

Maggie reached for Camila's hand. Her grip was strong with fear. Her other already rested on Charles's chest. Their hearts were beating. Their chests were rising. They were alive, and so was she.

Maggie plunged into the void, leaving her body in that horrible parlor where someone shouted her name. Maggie reached with such focus, such purpose. And even as she was surrounded by the utter dark, the freezing nothingness, she was warm. She was alive.

Among the whispering, she heard it. *Murder... murder... murderer.* Anne had fallen deep into the darkness of the Nether, but within that moment, it was as if they were standing face to face.

"Help us," Maggie breathed.

Their beings tied into one, not as it had been before, a hideous knot, but a perfect braid. They surfaced in the parlor together.

"Answer me!" Ruthie shrieked.

Camila was sobbing, still clinging to her hand. Jonathan clutched the mantle, heaving a desperate sigh of relief as Maggie opened her eyes.

"Maggie?" Walter asked.

Her focus did not drift to them as she maintained the bond, the careful balance between the warmth of the living and the icy touch of Anne's presence within her.

Camila screamed and Jonathan cursed as Ruthie was pulled from her feet. Her body lifted as suddenly as if she were indeed falling until she was pressed against the ceiling, emitting a string of sobbing screams, the rifle lying harmlessly on the rug beneath her.

"Maggie, what's-" Camila began but shrieked as the maid fell as suddenly as she had risen until she was limp on the ground.

"Get the gun!" Jonathan said, finally finding his words, though his face was totally white.

Walter, who was a good deal more collected, being more accustomed to such unusual sights, quickly grabbed the rifle. Ruthie stirred feebly, though it was clear that she was not moving anywhere soon.

Maggie exhaled a great sigh as she released Anne's spirit. In her lap, Charles stirred. "Anne," he whispered. Though as her eyes studied his face, he was no more conscious than before.

"Jonathan, come and help," Camila said.

Together he and Walter lifted Charles off of her gently and set him to lay on the rug. Maggie stood sorely. "Oh, Christ!" Maggie swore, limping. "My ankle."

Her brother helped her into the armchair, Maggie wincing at every movement.

"I should think we'll need an ambulance, and the police as well," Walter said.

"Yes, right," Jonathan agreed, nodding as he rested his hands on his hips.

"Shall I go and tell the front desk to phone them?"

"Yes," Jonathan said stiffly. "I'll remain here and... make sure all is in order."

"Very good," Walter said quickly, handing Jonathan the rifle and making his way out into the hall.

Without him, the parlor was quiet for several moments as Jonathan paced, Camila looked over Charles's body, and Maggie rubbed her forehead, trying to fight off possibly the worst headache of all time.

"It's just not possible," Jonathan muttered at last. "It simply isn't. We just-"

"You did it, didn't you?" Camila asked softly.

The room was silent as they both turned to her waiting in desperate silence for an explanation. It was a wholly complicated matter. Had Maggie lifted Ruthie's body from the floor? No. That had been entirely Anne's doing. But without Maggie, Anne would never have had the strength to, not in this place. Yet, she was sure that her spirit had been able to sense that Charles was in great danger. But that was just simply too much to explain to two very traumatised people, and her head hurt altogether too much to do anything more than nod.

"It's not possible," Jonathan said, though no matter how firm his manner was, it was clear that his certainty had cracked quite completely.

CHAPTER

15

MAGGIE CURLED HER FINGERS around the teacup's dainty handle, grimacing at the stretching sensation against her skin. Five days of bandages and ointments had done well to heal most of the burns, though the skin still felt oddly tight and uncomfortable. She wouldn't complain though. Anything to have the use of her fingers back.

Camila was watching her from the armchair. It was nice to have the company, though it would have been nicer if she wasn't under strict orders from Jonathan to make sure that Maggie remained sprawled on the couch for another day. Her dear brother had made sure she had spent hardly a moment alone since the incident. It had taken her only a day and a half to realise he had established some manner of shifts between her caretakers. Even Walter had come by twice to play nanny for him. They disguised this changing of the guard as chance happenings. *"Oh, I was just stopping by to look in."* *"Yes, well, I should be going anyway."* It was all horribly transparent really, but Maggie hadn't complained.

"I rather think June," Camila said, defaulting to one of their prime topics of conversation, the impending wedding.

Maggie nodded.

"Spring would just be too soon, wouldn't it?" she posed.

"June will be perfect," Maggie said. "It's a good month for travel. The flowers will be perfect, and there is nothing worse than rain on a wedding day."

"That is true, but-"

A knock on the door interrupted her thought. Camila looked toward the sound with a perplexed expression. Clearly, the next shift had arrived earlier than scheduled.

Maggie took another sip of her tea placidly as Camila stood to answer it.

"Oh," Camila said. The surprise in her voice drew Maggie's attention at once. "Please, come in."

Charles stepped through the door, his hat in hand. Their eyes connected as Camila shut the door behind him. He was wearing his black overcoat, thick snowflakes dusting the shoulders. Maggie had not seen him since that night at his apartment. Jonathan had categorically refused to escort her to visit him in the hospital. It had reportedly taken him several days to recover from the poison which had been laced into his scotch. Though no matter how much Maggie had wanted to visit, even simply to reassure herself that he was well, she quite honestly hadn't been in any fit state to do so.

"Charles," Maggie said, feeling suddenly aware of how unkempt she must appear from days of slouching in this very spot.

"How are you feeling?" he asked.

"Much better," Maggie said, pulling herself upright on the couch and stifling a betraying wince.

Charles's gaze fell down to his hat which she realised he was gripping rather tightly. "I was rather hoping that we could speak, you and I," he said.

"Of course," Maggie said. "We could go for a walk around the park."

"Maggie," Camila interceded. "Are you sure you're feeling up to it?"

"Quite sure," Maggie said, standing slowly. "I think a bit of fresh air is exactly what I need."

Camila nodded, agreeing apprehensively.

"Very well then," Charles said.

Maggie pulled on her coat, with Camila's assistance, and Charles followed her out the door.

Outside, it was a mild winter day, and though the air was cold, it was not forbiddingly so. The fresh air was every bit as wonderful as she had hoped. Still, they set a quick pace through the city streets, only slowing once they reached the boundaries of the park.

Maggie chanced a look up at Charles's face and saw his jaw set firmly, his gaze following his feet.

"I would ask you if you were alright, but I know that you can't be, not truly," Maggie said, letting out a long breath. "So instead, I will say that it's very good to see you."

He turned to her briefly with an arched brow. "It would be a lie to say that seeing you hasn't been the best part of these bitter days." They passed another couple huddled together for warmth, though otherwise, the paths were unusually sparse. "I was worried about you, though Walter kindly informed me that you were recovering well. I must confess that I couldn't help but come to see for myself."

"It was only a few burns," Maggie said. "Jonathan wrote our parents that I accidentally toppled a scalding kettle." Maggie laughed lightly, but Charles's brow remained tense over his dark eyes. "What is it?"

Charles sighed, looking away from her for a moment before he spoke, a movement that only fed the dread pooling in her chest. "Maggie, I- I've not been myself these past weeks. I haven't acted as I would expect of myself, or to the standard which you deserve."

"Charles, you've been through considerable hardship... heartbreak. I fault you for nothing. No one could," Maggie reassured.

"I do, Maggie," Charles insisted.

Maggie stopped, bringing her gaze to meet his. There was such misery in his eyes, and guilt too. She could not understand what for.

"I took terrible advantages-"

"No," Maggie stopped him, shaking her head. "Please don't. If that kiss was a mistake, then it was mine too. You took nothing from me that I did not freely give."

She reached her gloved hand for his own. He took it, letting out a deep sigh as he gave her a squeeze. Then let her go. Her arm felt heavy and awkward as she drew it back.

"I'm leaving, Maggie," he said, meeting her eye. "I'm going to stay with my family in Virginia."

"I see," Maggie breathed.

A bitter wind blew over her, the cold seeping through her coat.

"I've taken a leave of absence from the firm. My mother has been begging me to ever since..." He wiped a gloved hand over his mouth. "I'll be with family. I'll have time there. I need to find my life again, to find myself."

"I understand," Maggie said softly.

And she did. She had felt Anne's broken heart when their minds were joined within the house, the wrenching pain that tore from the inside out. She had watched Charles's face as he'd seen her in the flames. He'd loved her. Yet none of that kept the same clawing pain from seeding in her chest.

Maggie bit her lip, unable to stop herself.

"Maggie, I-" Pain choked at his voice. He shook his head irritably, looking for the words. "It was never my intention- I never wanted to hurt you. I only fear that if I stay...." His arms reached for her, but Maggie pushed them gently back to his sides.

"But you cannot," Maggie said firmly, to herself as much as him.

Charles drew in his lips and nodded to himself. "Tell me you won't hate me when I go. It's selfish of me, but-"

Maggie caught his eyes and pushed back the lump growing in her throat. "I couldn't," she promised. The icy wind stung at her eyes as she held his gaze until she could no longer. "Goodbye, Charles." She forced the words past her lips, and they came as nothing but a hoarse whisper.

She turned, following their footprints back through the snow, alone. It was only five steps before she had to cover her mouth to keep an unbidden sob from overtaking her. Maggie could feel his eyes on her back, even long after she knew he was far away, but she did not look back. Somehow, one foot after another, she made it back to Warren Street.

Maggie came through the door to the apartment, shutting it slowly behind her.

"Where is Charles?" Camila asked as Maggie began the painful process of removing her coat. "He didn't walk you home?"

"He's going home, to Virginia, to stay with family for a while," Maggie said as she hung her coat carefully. She crossed to the couch and sat down with a long sigh.

"I see," Camila said, sitting beside her.

"He just wanted to say goodbye," Maggie added.

Camila nodded knowingly. "He has only just lost his wife."

"You think I don't know that?" Maggie snapped, feeling instantly remorseful. "I'm sorry," she said, rubbing her face tensely. "I only meant to say that I doubt his leaving is any measure of his fondness for you," Camila reassured.

Maggie shook her head with a humorless laugh. "It's not even like I want-" she interrupted her own thought with a growl which turned to a low groan as her head fell into her hands.

To Camila's great credit, she said nothing but offered a comforting hand on her back until Maggie recovered herself.

"So, June then?" Maggie said finally.

"Yes, I do think so."

Some hours later, Camila left Maggie to her own devices. It had been all of a few moments before she could no longer stand the stillness. Walter found her up in the parlor, rather unexpectedly standing on her chair, dusting the trio of crows on the top of the wardrobe. Many of the books and curios had been removed from their usual space and stacked about the room.

"Oh dear," Walter said despite himself.

Maggie turned, startled by his apparently sudden appearance.

"Walter!" she greeted him with a smile, climbing down carefully.

"Are you alright?" he asked, still taking in the chaotic state of the once orderly parlor.

Maggie looked about with a small laugh. "It's a mess now, but the room was in need of a thorough tidying. I plan to begin hosting sittings again soon, and well, it's been a long time since I've had the chance. Our housekeeper refuses to clean up here, superstitions and all. Not to mention I've been on that damnable couch for days. I needed a project, something to do."

"Well, it is good to see you on your feet," Walter admitted. "I just hope you're not taking on too much too soon."

"I'm quite alright," Maggie said, turning to dust off a pile of tired looking books.

"I received a letter from our Mr. Blackbourne," Walter said to her back.

"He was by earlier today," she said without turning.

"It's a shame about his relocation," Walter said. "Though I was speaking with my superiors. I'm still gathering my findings, but this case has certainly gathered their interest."

"Really?" Maggie looked back at him, setting down the feather duster.

"Yes, they were singularly impressed by your involvement, I must say. Our collective findings could prove rather groundbreaking to the field."

"Walter, that's wonderful!"

A smile spread across his lips as her excitement infected him as well. "It could potentially mean publication, perhaps even notoriety by the scientific community at large."

"My goodness," Maggie said, quite lost for words. Of all the things she had imagined for herself, being published in a scientific journal had never been among them, but even so, a swell of pride filled her.

"I was hoping to speak with you today, about perhaps continuing our partnership," Walter proposed hesitantly.

"In what capacity?"

"Well, I suppose that is up for discussion. I had thought to observe some of your sittings, perhaps even run scientific tests in my own offices, to better understand your process."

"Of course."

"I was also thinking, that if, well, another case of significance were to present itself, we might be able to provide assistance, together."

Maggie was quiet a moment, considering.

"I think that we did such a service with the Blackbourne case," he continued. "The spirit put to rest, the true killer caught and behind bars, not to mention the wealth of knowledge gathered. The destruction of the property was, of course unfortunate…"

"Yes," Maggie said finally.

"Yes?"

"This is why I began hosting sittings in the first place, to help people, and to learn about myself," Maggie explained. "Our work together, it allows us to do both on such a scale."

"Very well then," Walter said, adjusting his glasses with a smile.

Maggie could not help but grin back. This was what she wanted, what she craved, this wonderful feeling of being filled with magnificent purpose.

Acknowledgments

Firstly, I want to thank my husband, Zack Applewhite for picking my writing up out of the trash and always made sure my coffee was warm.

Of course, I owe a huge debt to my beta readers: Stephanie Chapa, Charles Hegedus, Laura Hendricks, Eric Jenkins, Holly Taylor, and Paul Turner. You helped me shape this story into a book.

I am forever grateful to the 210 Kickstarter backers who supported this book including my patron backers: Simon Felline, Elizabeth Cox, Jim "Hawkmir" Deyo, Jennifer Harlin, Sherry Mock, Larry Williams, Iris Pleitez, Joseph Grim II, Kaitlyn Bartchak-Cathcart, and Stephanie Chapa. My first readers will always have a special place in my heart.

A very special thanks to my kids who suffered through many arduous mornings of cartoons and goldfish so that Mommy could be herself. I hope that one day you follow your own dreams while your kids scream at you from the other room that they're hungry… again.

To my cats who sat with me(on me) through every stage of this process.

To Marabel, you inspired me, and Camila.

COMING 2024

Piercing *The* Veil

Book Two in the White Crow Series by

KALYNN APPLEWHITE

Sample Chapter

MAGGIE STEPPED OUT ONTO the sidewalk. She could already hear the calls from the steps of city hall. A wave of excitement washed over her, and Camila came to her side. Arm in arm, they rushed to join the others. There was a great diversity gathered. Old women beside young. A few had even brought little ones wrapped snugly in their carriages or held on hips. Some were dressed in the latest fashions. Others were clearly of more meager means, but it hardly mattered. They were united under the colors of the movement, purple, white, and gold, worn on sashes or buttons over their long woolen coats. Others carried signs painted with messages such as *"Equal rights for all!"* and *"Don't deny us our democratic duties!"*. Lest it escape anyone's attention their purpose, a large banner was planted beside the emblazoned with VOTES FOR WOMEN.

"It's already taken hold in the West!" a woman shouted down to those who passed below. "We can bring suffrage to the East! Votes for Women!" The speaker set her sights on a man passing on the street. "Sir- your daughters deserve the right to control their destinies!"

The man stopped and regarded her with a polite nod before continuing on his way.

"Votes for Women!" Camila called loudly as they joined the others.

The speaker turned to her with a wide smile. "Camila!" she greeted, her voice somewhat hoarse.

They shared a brief hug before the speaker turned to Maggie. She was older than they were by some years. Friendly laugh lines marked her eyes. A touch of grey was coming to her hair. "You must be Margaret."

"Maggie, please."

The speaker nodded. "We've got sashes just here," she said, pointing to a picnic basket on the steps behind her.

Soon, they both wore a sash trimmed with purple and gold.

And then it began. The speakers rotated, to spare the voices. They called endlessly, sometimes picking out passersby, especially those on their way into city hall. More than once, a woman had heard their calls and joined their number. More than once, someone had called for them to go home, or some such unsavory sentiment, men and women alike. It strained logic as to why any woman of sound mind would want to limit herself. The speaker, whoever it was, never engaged with the naysayers and that was ample medicine to see them soon disperse, even if Maggie would have preferred to wring some of their necks instead.

It was more than two hours, and one small spot of rain later, that Camila was given the role of speaker. Maggie stood at her side, answering all calls faithfully. From Main Street around the corner, Maggie caught sight of a policeman speaking with an aggrieved man in a suit. She watched as he indicated clearly in their direction.

Maggie elbowed Camila purposefully, directing her attention as a second officer joined the first. She only gave a slight nod, indicating that she understood, and then raised her voice. "…and as all men are created equal, women are not their subservients. All are equal in the sight of God as it should be in the law!"

As the officers came to the steps, Maggie squared her shoulders. If the others were standing their ground, she was not going to back down.

"Alright!" the younger of the two boomed. "You've said your piece. It's time to go on home now."

"We have the right to assemble!" Camila shouted for the benefit of the passerby. "Our constitution-"

"This disturbance must disperse-"

"Votes for Women!" someone in the crowd bellowed.

His face was naturally ruddy but reddened into a deep, violent shade. "That's enough," he said, grabbing Camila by the wrist.

Camila let out a little shriek of surprise as Maggie pushed herself between them. "You let go of her," she demanded.

Behind her, one of the children started to cry.

The officer rounded on her angrily just as the older of the two put his hand on his shoulder, giving him a stern look. After a moment, he unhanded Camila who eyed him venomously.

"Ladies," the older voiced loudly. However, his tone conveyed only passive annoyance at the situation. "You can disperse now, or we can take you in and yer husbands can come deal with ya. Choice is yours."

Maggie and Camila stood arm against arm, leaning on the metal bars of the holding cells. Beyond were a dozen or so desks, most of which were empty. The others were manned by officers who, every now and then, would glance back to see if they had broken. It was as if admitting how tired they all were or complaining about the wretched smell, or rude remarks from their drunken neighbors in the neighboring cell, or the three hours they had been made to wait without contacting their families would be allowing the enemy to win.

At home, Jonathan was likely tying himself in a knot by now that they had not returned. The possibility of making it to her dinner with George was becoming more remote by the minute. Of course, an evening in this dismal cell would be arguably preferable if it would not put her in even hotter water where her parents were concerned. The situation was not one she wished to aggravate, nor her poor brother's nerves. Of course, she did not want to be the one who broke the silent vigil of her fellow ladies. But Maggie had also had quite enough of being stuffed into the cramped cell like a sardine in a can.

What she did next was neither dignified nor altogether mature, but desperate times... Maggie waited until a particular officer was passing by. He was younger than most of the others, with soft, boyish features. He'd been looking back at them more often than the rest, with a hint of sympathy in his eyes. Calling upon every bit of drama within herself, Maggie swooned, falling to the ground amid a cloud of startled gasps.

Within seconds she could feel a dozen hands fanning her face as she lay there, limp as a fish. Outside, Maggie could hear the young officer undoing the lock.

"Step aside. Give her some air," he said chivalrously.

My hero, Maggie thought, schooling her brow into a pain crease.

"Is she alright?" Camila said anxiously.

Maggie opened her eyes blearily, looking at the many faces peering down at her.

"Are you alright, miss?" he asked.

"Yes," Maggie said faintly. "It must have been the heat. I have such a weak constitution. I'm so sorry."

Camila helped her slowly to her feet, and Maggie wobbled unsteadily to reinforce her charade.

"Come with me," he said. "We'll get you some water."

Maggie looked back at the others as if conflicted before nodding, following the officer out of the holding cell, and taking a breath of mercifully fresh air.

"Is there someone you can call to come and get you?" he said, offering her a chair beside his desk. His blue eyes were clear and wide.

"My brother," Maggie said. "He'll be so worried about us."

"Of course, write the number here, and I will notify him."

Maggie smiled and nodded as she scribbled the number onto the paper. The young officer took the paper and promised to return with a glass of water. When he was gone, Maggie offered a brief nod to Camila who returned it knowingly.

As she waited, Maggie's curious eyes wandered over the officer's desk, but all the papers were on disappointedly mundane matters. Yet the desk just behind her was much busier. Thick folders were piled on one another at odd angles. Maggie glanced around the room, but none of the men were paying her any particular attention. She flicked open one of the folders.

At once, Maggie felt a prickle over her skin. She heard the whispering of the void, and her focus honed. Resting on the top of several files was a velvet choker. A single stone rested in the center. It was clearly a costume piece. The gem was scratched in many places, the velvet worn from use. Yet, Maggie could not take her eyes off it. A single voice was emerging from the mist. The police station was fading from her mind as she reached for the necklace.

The stone against her skin was like ice. At once, Maggie was plunged into the darkness. She gasped, but the frigid air caught in her throat. Panic beat against her chest. She couldn't breathe. Distantly she could feel herself falling, but her focus was shifting away from her own consciousness. The whispering presence was still circling her. Maggie clung to it in desperation.

Suddenly, she was grasping at sheets as she lay in a bed not her own. She couldn't breathe. Strong hands were pushing down on her neck. The stone of her necklace was cutting into her throat. No, not hers. Maggie told herself, but reason was nothing to her as she fought for air.

Her eyes darted around, looking for someone, anyone, to stop this. The room was covered in faded floral wallpaper, which was waterstained and peeling in many places. Even the sheet beneath her was damp in the corner by her head. There was a door in the very corner of her vision, but it was shut and silent. It was hard to see much more as the hands around her neck held her firm. Her lips formed silent pleas as she stared at the door. No one came.

She seemed to accept that no one would come as she gripped the arms of her attacker, fingers digging into his skin in desperation. Then she saw it, that face. His veins were strained on his temple, grey eyes wide and angry. Maggie's scream caught in her throat. She thrashed and clawed as darkness began to crowd her vision.

Then she felt it, beneath her hand, the beat of a living heart. Maggie pulled herself toward its warmth with all her will.

The material plane collided with her senses as Maggie gasped for precious air. She had fallen to the floor, a number of faces now distorted on the edges of her vision. She was gripping the arm of an officer so tightly her knuckles were white. His other hand rested on her shoulder as his clear blue eyes studied her face from beneath his drawn brow. He was a stranger to her. His jaw was rounded and clean shaven. A few longs of reddish brown hair had fallen into his face. Maggie found herself locked in his gaze as she gulped down air, feeling the beat of his heart. It beat ardently, strong and defiant of the coldness beyond, anchoring her.

"It was him!"

Printed in Great Britain
by Amazon

27226559R00121